jason myers

MW00943891

Skullburn '77
(who am i?)

also by jason myers:

novels:
exit here.
the mission
dead end
run the game
blazed
a sad history of beautiful nostalgia (skullburn '78)

novellas:
destroy

www.exitheremediasf.com

skullburn

(who am i?)

'77

I dedicate this book with very special thanks to:

My kickass editor and newbie on the literature scene, Katelyn Nelson. Watch out world, she's gonna be special!

And to all the radical, beautiful and brilliant kids I ran wild through the streets of SF with from 2002-2006.
Thank you for three lifetimes worth of experiences and stories. And thank you so much for having the audacity to get me to start thinking that I might be able to actually cut it as an artist. Y'all were so amazing.
The kings and queens of the city's last great era of art.

And finally, this book is dedicated to all my dear friends who've passed away the last two years.
I fucking miss you so much.

"All writers are vain, selfish and lazy, and at the very bottom of their motives there lies a mystery."

-George Orwell

"I relish my debauchery. I don't regret it or shy away from it and pretend that I'm gonna stop it. This is who I am, and I'm not going to change for anyone."

-James Morgan

"A love like that was a serious illness, an illness from which you never entirely recover."

-Charles Bukowski

1.

"Over and over I keep going over the world we knew...Once when you walked beside me...That inconceivable, that unbelievable world we knew..."

There's a familiar heaviness, a kind of beautiful sadness in my heart when I wake up with these Frank Sinatra lyrics swirling through my head.

Natasha whispers something in her sleep before turning on her side and instead of waking her up and screwing her, I decide to live in this melancholy rush, a gift from my dreams I suppose, and I carefully step out of bed and walk to the window and light a cigarette.

It's my last morning in Los Angeles and everything is perfect.

Right now at least.

As I look over my shoulder at that beautiful girl and Frank Sinatra sings...

"When we two were in love..."

2.

Up on the rooftop of The Standard Hotel in downtown Los Angeles, I lay in a chaise lounge and drink from the bottle of champagne I bought, staring at a group of three incredibly gorgeous women in their bikinis from underneath my shades.

Natasha, she's still sleeping in my room on the fifth floor.

My phone buzzes and I reach down and grab it off the towel I'd set it on and immediately wish I hadn't.

On the screen is a text message from my ex-girlfriend, Allison, which is written to appear like a group text.

But it's so not.

There are no other names or numbers attached.

It goes:

Hey everyone! As you all know, I turned 28 today. OMG! I can barely believe it myself. So I guess there's only one thing to do...CELEBRATE! To kick the night off, a bunch of us are getting together at Farmer Brown's at five for happy hour. After that, the party moves to Sushi Rock for dinner and more drinking. From there, we move to Tempest and from there, who the fuck knows! We'll let the night take us where it wants to. Hope to see all of your faces at some point. These last six months have been the best six months of my life. Let's do this! Let's make my 28th birthday magical!

I light a cigarette and pound another swig.

I know exactly what she's up to with this text.

That last six months bullshit.

I broke up with Allison for good six months ago.

On August 14th to be exact.

She wants to break into my head and steal my day by forcing me to contemplate the notion of her life being so much more amazing since our split.

She wants me to care but I don't.

About her birthday this year, I don't.

But I do care about my history with her.

Our story.

I do care that on this day last year, I executed her 27th birthday to perfection and we had so much fucking fun.

This happened before I found out she was a lying whore and a fucking disaster.

Before I realized she was an evil cunt.

This text would actually piss me off if it wasn't so transparent with her desire to make me jealous by getting me to wonder about who she's going to be with and if tonight will be better than tonight last year.

I delete the text and look at the time.

Eleven-thirty.

Almost time to go.

Which sucks, and leads to this brutal feeling of emptiness that sweeps right through me and upsets me.

I mean, this is so close to paradise.

The warmth.

And sun.

And women.

And champagne.

The bullet of cocaine in the pocket of my swimming trunks.

And my gorgeous, nineteen year old lover, Natasha, naked and asleep in my room.

Three days I've been in L.A., which is the perfect amount of time.

Anything less and I always feel a little cheated and underwhelmed.

Anything more though, and I end up tip-toeing around the sharp edges of madness, self-loathing, and a fierce kind of cynicism that's capable of rendering me useless for a few days after I leave.

As I twist out my cigarette, I open Facebook and the first three posts I see are about my favorite bar in the city, the Tiger Kill, and how it's closing for good after tonight.

Another casualty of the tech and real estate industry's blatant assault on the Mission, which used to be the best neighborhood in the country (in my opinion).

The Tiger Kill is one of the three bars where I really cut my teeth after moving to San Francisco to study film twelve years ago (Arrow Bar and the Hemlock being the others).

It's the first bar I ever had sex in.

And the only place I've ever been allowed to dump a bunch of cocaine onto the bar and spell my name with it.

Plus, it's where my first band in San Francisco, GrundlePig, played our first show.

Knowing that I'll be able to get one more night in this magical haunt makes me feel much better now about the text and leaving.

What also makes me feel better is this: sliding the bullet out, loading it, and smashing blow up my nose.

I do it four times.

Then I finish off the bottle of champagne and close out my tab.

"What was the name on the card again?" the bartender asks me as my phone buzzes again with another text from Allison.

This one though, it's really for me and me only.

And it says:

I'm so sorry. I didn't mean for you to get that last text. I would never want you to know that I'm going to Farmer Brown's, Sushi Rock, and Tempest for my birthday. Please disregard that itinerary if you read it. Wasn't for you.

I roll my eyes and smirk.

Bitch ain't fooling no one.

Last I heard, she was moving in with some flute playing asshole with a trust fund and a soul patch.

"Sir," the bartender says.

Fuck her.

And fuck him.

I look back up. "Yes."

"The name on the card, sir. What was it?"

Fuck them all.

I win.

"Oh yeah," I say. "Sorry about that."

"No problem at all. I just need your name."

"Myers," I say. "Jason Myers."

3.

Natasha is sliding her pink lace underwear on when I enter the room.

Frowning at me, she goes, "Where were you?"

"The roof," I tell her. "I wanted one last hurrah up there."

She smiles but it's forced.

She's sad that I'm leaving soon.

And so am I.

I love this girl.

And this girl loves me.

We've been in love for a year but there's nothing we can do to improve the situation.

We live in different cities, different worlds, which is a reality that's difficult just to contemplate transforming.

She's so young and there's so much she needs to do and see. There really is.

But me, I'm thirty-three and I've been all over and experienced so much it feels like too much at times.

It's not just that I feel like I've lived twice the life of my age, it's that I have lived it, and that burning desire to keep chasing it down and drinking it all up isn't there.

At least right now.

And even if she did move to San Francisco (something we've discussed many times) it wouldn't be at all like the way we romanticize it in our heads.

My guess is that we'd fall apart very quickly.

I'd never be okay with her doing the shit I believe you have to do at her age and in that city.

My anger would turn to hate.

I know myself well enough to understand that.

After I pop the cap off the Red Stripe I take out of the mini fridge, I go, "Do you have any of those Valiums left?"

Natasha nods. "There's at least ten left, Jason. Do you want them?"

"A few at least."

She's putting on her bra now and I go to her and slide my hand around her waist. Her arms drop to the sides and I stare into her beautiful green eyes.

"It's Allison's birthday today."

Natasha's cheeks instantly turn bright red and she smacks my hand away and turns around.

"What?" I sigh. "I was with her for almost three years, but I never loved her the way I love you."

"Bullshit."

"I don't think it is."

Facing me again, she goes, "Why would you bring her up right before you leave? Fuck her birthday, dude. The things she did to you...the hell she put you through."

"It wasn't always like that."

"No relationship stays the way it was in the awesome beginning of it. You know this. You write about this in some of your books."

"I know."

Natasha looks at me with absolute disgust as she grabs her purse off the nightstand and digs through it.

I light a cigarette and walk over to the desk to get my phone so I can play her a song to offset my sin of bringing up Allison.

It was a terrible move but I thought irritating her might make me feel better cos here's the deal:

In twenty minutes, me and her are going to be holding hands as we leave the room and walk down the hallway and ride the elevator to the lobby. Then while we wait for the valet to fetch the car I rented, we'll be insanely making out in between confirming how much we love one another. And once I finally kiss her for the last time and let go of her hands, I'm driving six hours home while she's taking a cab to the Hollywood apartment she shares with her boyfriend.

This is the deal!

But it didn't help at all.

What I did.

I feel like shit for doing it so now I play her a song.

It's Coltrane's "In A Sentimental Mood" and when I turn around, Natasha is standing inches from me with five Valiums in her hand.

"Goddamn, I love you," I tell her then take them from her and set them on the desk.

"I love you, too."

"Oh yeah?"

She's smiling again. "Yeah."

Grabbing ahold of her by the waist, I pull her off the ground and she wraps her legs around me while we kiss with the kind of passion no writer could ever capture with the proper set of words.

Seconds later, after I've laid her on the bed, I'm ripping her underwear off then pushing her legs further apart then sliding my jeans down while she scoots further up the bed.

"Get inside of me now," she says.

I do.

And it ends up being the best goddamn sex of the whole fucking trip.

4.

It's almost eight as I'm guiding the car off the freeway and onto the Civic Center exit, only a few blocks from my apartment on 8th and Bryant where I've lived for the last two years. Since I don't have to return the car until tomorrow, I park it in the alley next to my pad which sits right above this delicious restaurant, Henry Hunan's.

I have three roommates, all of whom I get along fairly well with, and none of whom are here right now.

And this pleases me.

I unlock my bedroom door and flip the lights on.

Light a cigarette.

Before I begin the never simple task of unpacking, I kneel down and start flipping through a crate of my vinyl, which consumes much more time than I thought it would.

Twenty minutes later, I finally make a choice.

A very strong one too.

I've chosen *Songs From The Big Chair*, the second record by Tears For Fears, and right after "Shout" begins to blast from the speakers, I pump my fist into the air then plug in my phone, which has been dead for over five hours, into the charger.

I could've charged it in the car but chose not to after I received another text from Allison that read:

Seriously, Jason. Nothing at all??? You asked me to marry you once while you were rolling on Molly and doing blow and I was so high that I said yes. But the second you sobered up, you began to distance yourself from your insane proposal until I just let you off the hook by telling you I wasn't ready to be married. Fuck you! You're a fucking joke. Plus I really hated all that Das Racist you played like every night we hung out during our last month together. And oh, that last month, the one where you ditched me over seven times so you could sit in your room alone and watch Michigan football and basketball games from the early nineties on YouTube, that month was the worst month of my life. Just fuck you.

Shit makes me laugh even though she's not lying.

Pause.

Actually, now that I think about it again, I don't think she disliked Das Racist that much. And I certainly didn't play them as much as she claimed.

So really, she is lying a little bit.

And it still makes me laugh.

I walk over to my desk and twist off the top of the bullet and dump out the final remnants of cocaine from the massive and strange purchase I made on my first night in L.A.

My homie, Roland, the lead singer of the seminal noise-thrash-punk band, Dark Beauty, picked me up at the Standard and drove me to this bungalow in Silver Lake.

The scene was wild.

Right as we arrived, this Asian dude with long gray hair and face tattoos answered the door wearing a pink silk bathrobe. Wrapped around his waist was a leather belt with a holster and gun, which he ended up waving around at least six times while we were there.

The Lost Highway *soundtrack was fucking blasting.*

He led us into this large room and there were two young, beautiful girls in lingerie sprawled out on separate couches. A bit of uneasiness traveled through me as my eyes swung back and forth between them like a pendulum.

It was sorta creepy but kinda hot.

Their eyes were glossy and I don't recall either of them moving.

Images of me fucking them while they choked me as hard as they could smashed through my head.

A glass table sat between the couches.

Two drug shooting kits laid on top of it along with a brick of H and a brick of cocaine.

Immediately, my mind switched gears as my eyes locked on the awesomeness of the bricks.

I was fucking salivating.

Drooling as I stared at my own kind of heaven.

The Asian man hugged Roland more than once and asked many questions about his band. Me, I was totally ignored (something I was very okay with) until my friend decided to mention that I was a somewhat successful author with four published novels.

This made me cringe and I glared hard at Roland as all the energy and attention in the room quickly focused on me and I began to get ready to answer the usual questions that always follow this revelation.

1. What are my books about?
2. How long does it take me to write a book?
3. Do I have any of my books on me?
4. If I was going to buy one (which I'm totally not) which one should I start with?
5. Did I always want to be a writer?
6. How should I go about getting the book I've been thinking about writing for three years published?
7. Will you read it if I write it and send it to you?
8. Can you send me copies of your book when you get some more?
9. Have you ever read (insert like ten books and authors here)?
10. I've really been focusing on trying to write more lately but mostly it's been poetry. Can I send you those?
11. Is it hard for you to write your books?
12. How much time should I spend a day writing? It seems more consuming than I thought it would be.
13. My ideas are insane and I really think it would be the best book ever but how you do you know if what you're writing will get published?
14. Should I even finish the book before I start sending it out?

I was so annoyed at first.

I'm always annoyed when heavily doped up and intoxicated people find out that I'm a published author because I always get trapped by them.

Like they get right in my face and demand to know how it works and how it happened for me...

I sat down for months at a time and wrote the damn things, asshole. And then I figured it out from there.

But the Asian man didn't want any answers. He just waved his gun around and asked me for my email address. I wrote it down and he gave me a hug and then ordered my fourth novel, Run The Game *on his Android.*

*I ended up buying eight grams of coke and he
threw in a small sack of H just for the hell of it.*

*He also told me that if one of the "sweet dolls" on
the couches actually wanted to fuck me that night, he'd be
more than happy to let me get it.*

*"But the thing is, Jason," he said while twirling the
gun around his finger. "They fucking love me and me only.
I can't get them off of my hands. Most of the time, they
refuse to talk to anyone else at all. They think it's an act of
betrayal."*

"How's the sleeping arrangement work?" I asked.

*"Great question," the Asian man said. "I've got this
huge, Georgian poster bed in the master bedroom. It's the
most beautiful piece of furniture you'll ever see. I was in
Charleston, South Carolina meeting a front about some
jewels I was in possession of. Me and the girls, we stayed
in this bed and breakfast. A gorgeous place. And that was
the bed in our room. The owner didn't want to sell it at
first but I'm one of those guys, ya know."*

"What guys?"

*"Guys who don't take no for an answer. There is
always currency for yes. You just have to find it.*

Me and my friend did a bump.

*And mister bathrobe said, "I sleep in the middle
and my girls, they sleep right next to me with guns
clutched in their hands."*

"Rad."

*After another bump, we split. But not before the
gun came out a final time and the man said, "After you
sign the book and send it back to me, if you want, I will
make one of my angels get on a plane to San Francisco
regardless of how she feels about it and you can have her
for a week."*

*He went, "I only ask that you never kiss her, don't
fall in love with her, and only use duct tape to tie her up
during intercourse. No rope. No fucking handcuffs. Just
tape. Only duct tape."*

5.

What I finally choose to wear out tonight is this: a black Get Dead tank top (not only are they one of my favorite bands of the past decade, responsible for two of my favorite records of all time, *Letters Home* & *Tall Cans & Loose Ends*, I go back to the beginning of my SF life with a couple of those dudes). I also choose a pair of skin tight, black Levi jeans, a pair of black leather loafers, and the brown Members Only jacket that I got by taking it right off this real turd burglar, this total d-bag, Travis Fuller, while he was passed out in a booth at the 500 Club like six years ago because he owed four hundred dollars to Tatum Hurley, this chick I was banging at the time, and refused to pay her back so I just ripped the jacket off and gave her the twenty-three dollars and the like half of a half gram that was in one of the pockets.

I think she even blew me in Dolores Park later that night.

Or maybe it was in the chick's bathroom at the Uptown.

Coulda been both actually.

Prolly was both too.

Anyway, I've had this jacket ever since that night and I adore it and smile every time I put it on.

I snort another line of blast while that Wipers song, "Youth Of America" explodes from the speakers.

My phone dings.

It's a text from Ryan, my number one coke guy in the city.

It says that he's at the Kilowatt with some friends and that he hasn't been there in awhile and barely recognizes it right now.

It reads:

"*All I see are these juiced up, tech jocks with the same shitty moustaches, the same shitty Hitler haircuts, and they're wearing their v-necks wrong, dude. They're wearing them with shitty plaid scarves. And the girls here right now? I wanna slam all of their shitty faces through the jukebox and then steal their shitty leggings and tights and flats and their shiny fluorescent colored high tops and try to give it all to the homeless people walking by, but I* don't even think they'd want it. Who are these assholes? This is the Kilowatt, man! I used to come here just to see the new t-shirts the Melvins were selling on tour. Or if I wanted to get into a Chuck Mosely, Faith No More days sing-a-long with other people who've been stuck in a bathroom with Jello Biafra before, listening to him ramble for thirty minutes without ever knowing what the hell he was talking about."

This text is brilliant.

And I text Ryan that I'll be there soon and call a cab.

It's almost time to go.

After I spray some cologne on, I gulp down at least three shots worth of Maker's Mark, wipe my lips, and then smash the last Los Angeles rail up my nose as the Wipers sing...

The rich get richer and the poorer get poorer...Now there's no place left to go...Got to get off this rot...Man, this just ain't no existence...Beware of those guys in disguise...

6.

Sweat pours out of me in the back of the cab, so I open up a window and stick my head out of it as the nerves about going out solo begin to fill up in my gut. Obviously, all the coke I've blasted has a lot to do with what's happening, but with each block the driver blows by, I'm regretting my decision of rolling out solo, which in itself is a pretty fucking foreign feeling for me to have.

Mostly, I prefer to be alone. I began to notice this about six years ago and ever since then, this preference has only grown stronger and stronger and stronger.

I'm never bored.

Despite the fact that I have no new book in the actual draft stage, the ideas for three or four are there, they are. They're so there and two of them are damn near ready for pre-production.

I've got hundreds of pages of notes jotted down and I've been reading incessantly (a lot of scripts and political non-fiction) as I attempt to construct a plan for myself in case *Blazed* really is my final book (it's the last one I'm under contract for).

I mean, since I'm insanely jacked up right now, I might as well be super, duper honest about what's actually going on with me.

And it's this:

I am fucking terrified!

My life scares the hell out of me right now.

I'm thirty-three years old and my books are the closest thing to a "reliable" source of income that I have and this is now developing into a major issue for me because my popularity as an author is now in a fairly steady decline.

It's been going this way since *The Mission* was published even though I believe, as does my agent, that my last two books, *Dead End* and *Run The Game*, were so much more impressive and well written than the first two.

Especially *Run The Game*.

I'm still in a state of disbelief about how not well that book has sold.

Since I don't do a lot of media appearances anymore, a lot of people don't know much about me outside of the randomness of my Facebook posts or tweets. But *Run The Game*, that's the book I'd been waiting my whole life to write. The three books that came before it were just preparation for the story of Alexander Franklin and Patti Smith. Everything I've always thought a great novel should contain, *Run The Game* contained it and better yet, I was able to narrate that story through Alexander seamlessly.

I mean, I've never been in more control of a voice or a story despite how often it appeared to be totally out of control and overwhelmed by the chaos it was creating.

But it never was.

Not even close.

I was able to blow the lives of those kids up over and over, only to corral it right back in with ice cream cones on a busted merry go round or Chinese food and a Heart cassette tape.

I never expected the critics to like the book.

It's an incredibly raw and rough story, narrated in a very unrefined and unapologetic voice.

But I did expect people to admire it.

I thought they'd appreciate the guts and the honesty and the authenticity of the world I'd created.

I was convinced it was going to sell well but it hasn't.

For the first time, I think, there's been a line drawn in the sand with one of my books and you either adore *Run The Game* or you fucking hate *Run The Game* and if you're one of the ones who hate it, more than likely you have some animosity towards me (even if you loved the first three books) so the pressure is on *Blazed* (which really isn't fair to those characters) and the pressure is on me too now. To figure this shit out again and get back to where I was not that long ago.

"Baby," Natasha said on my first night in Los Angeles.

We were at Rivabella for dinner. She'd never been and I wanted to show off for her and I wanted to show her off as well so I made reservations three weeks before my trip and surprised her.

She marveled for most of the beginning part of the night. She was thrilled and she was so appreciative I'd done this for her. It's one of the things I love about her. She truly appreciates what she has (with me anyway) and what she gets from me even though she truly doesn't expect all that much from me.

It was after the bill came, and after I sent it back with my credit card, that I fell into a quiet daze which prompted her to go, "What's wrong?"

I finally looked back up at her and went, "I don't know."

"Baby," she said, then reached across the table and put her hand over mine. "Don't shut down on me, please."

When she squeezed my hand she smiled, and the warmth from that smile and those amazing fucking eyes and the comfort of her skin against mine, it was exactly what I needed to feel and to see.

And I went, "I just can't stop thinking about what happened."

"What do you mean, babe?"

"To me," I say. "My life. My career."

"You say that like you no longer have those things."

"Cos I don't," I tell her. "It's all gone. The money and the good sales and the comfort and stability. It's all gone."

"Come on, Jason," she says. "Your new book's coming out soon. You tell me it's the best thing you've done so far. That sounds like a pretty good life to me."

I pulled my hand away after she said that. I wasn't mad or irritated by what she'd said. I wasn't.

But it wasn't anything she could understand without me breaking it all down for her which wasn't something I was going to do.

Fuck that.

Relive it for what?

It's fucking done.

It's over.

And if there's anything I learned from writing *Exit Here*, it's that you can never go back.

7.

The Kilowatt.

I'm waiting for a shot of tequila and a Corona and I don't see Ryan anywhere so I text him and wait.

Standing next to me is this chick with long blonde hair and blue eyes. She looks like she'd do decent in porn.

"I love your hand tats," she tells me, inching a little bit closer to me as well.

"I don't," I say.

She frowns. "Why'd you get them then?"

"I was high," I tell her. "Both times."

She laughs. "Weed can bring out the randomness in me too," she says.

"What are you talking about?" I snort, as the bartender sets my drinks down.

"You said you were high."

"Yeah."

"Okay."

"On cocaine," I say.

"Oh."

"It's an ambitious sorta drug," I tell her. "Not like weed."

"I know," she says. "I've done coke."

"That's disgusting," I say. "That drug is awful."

The girl makes a face and hurriedly walks away, leaving me alone.

I take a deep breath now.

That band Fun! is playing on the jukebox.

If there was a spare brick sitting anywhere near me right now, Fun! would be shut the fuck down, my ears would stop bleeding, and I'd make damn sure that whichever asshole or butt faced blackout regret of a girl who chose this song picked up every broken piece, every shard of glass off the floor, while I stood over them and explained about making good choices going forward.

I'd tell them, "Your absurd salaries can buy you a lot of nice shit. Nice pussy and nice dick. Nice toys. Nice views. But the thing it can't buy you is authenticity and genuine cool. The most important thing a person can have. That kind of money can't make you into the real thing. Never has been able to and never will."

Ryan was right about this place in his text. I'm looking around and it's a far cry from the bar that I remember seeing Coachwhips and 400 Blows shred in 2004.

A few feet away from me there's this table and everyone at the table has their faces buried in their phones and there's this guy standing on the other side of me with two girls who look as boring as their jobs and I think I hear the guy say something about how much better a beer feels when you've worked such a long day and earned it. Both girls nod.

"Work hard, play hard," one of the girls then says before yawning.

At the very least, she deserves to be punched for saying that.

My phone buzzes after I down my shot. It's Ryan and that fucking cocksucker left and went to The Knockout.

I slam like half my beer then walk outside, light a cigarette, and call him.

"Dude," I say. "Why the fuck did you tell me to come to the Kilowatt if you were just going to leave?"

"You took too long, man. Besides, I couldn't stay in there any longer. It felt like the coding marathon was about to start or something. I was just waiting for Edward Sharpe and The Magnetic Zeros to start looping."

"Totally," I say. Then, "Who's playing at The Knockout?"

"This band Asphyxiated, dude. And they're fucking great."

"What time do they play?"

"Doesn't matter," he says. "Just get here."

"I wanna hit the Tiger Kill too, man. It's their last night ever."

"Oh, we're definitely hitting that," he says. "Just come to the Knockout though. You gotta see this band Asphyxiated first."

"Word."

Click.

I take a drag and look to my right and my goddamn heart squeezes up as my throat tightens.

I'm staring at Tokyo-A-Go-Go.

Fuck.

This is where I took Allison for dinner on her birthday last year.

Images of that day slam through my head.

Me waking up an hour before Allison and making her breakfast served with mimosas.

Me fucking Allison from behind.

Me handing her the first present of the day: A Marc Jacobs watch.

Me fucking her on her living room floor after she'd already gotten ready for work.

Pain and hurt like this, the way I feel inside as I stand here looking at the restaurant right now, it's something of a pleasure too. That day was magical, or at least it felt magical.

I love my nostalgia 99.9 percent of the time. It's basically just another one of my addictions now.

For weeks after Allison and I broke up, I buried myself under a stack of memories the two of us had created.

Movies we'd watched together.

The market near her house we bought our wine and snacks from.

Restaurants we ate at.

Bus and train routes we took to get to the destinations where some of our best fucking moments together occurred.

Some people when they break up, a lot of people actually, they go out of their way to avoid anything that could potentially trigger a relapse into the bottle of memories and emotions they're so desperately committed to never drinking from again.

I've never understood that.

Being held in the warm arms of my nostalgia has always been something I've taken great comfort and safety in.

There's something very fucking beautiful and calming about it. I really trust myself and perhaps that's why I'm not afraid of embracing parts of a particular

history I shared with someone who once meant a great
deal to my life.

I know I'm never going to back to her, to that. I
trust myself to know that it's over for good, for forever.

I also realize how little of my life is actually spent
feeling intoxicated from those perfect fucking moments me
and her created while the rest of my life is happily
embracing the joy and the relief of not being with her
anymore and not living through the unhappiness that had
begun to dominate the majority of our time together.

Even though I should be jumping into a cab and
hurrying to the Knockout, I decide instead to go into the
restaurant and at the very least, drink some Sake.

Maybe I'll even order a roll or two.

I know Allison is only a couple of blocks away from
me right now.

And I know that a part of her, some fucking piece
of her wants me to be with her tonight.

Wants me to celebrate with her.

So this is the best I can do.

This is me celebrating her birthday this year by
hanging out with the memory of the girl I thought she was,
the girl I fell in love with, the happy, caring, honest girl
that walked into this place on my arm a year ago.

Cheers to her.

And cheers to that beautiful fucking girl.

Wherever she is.

Wherever the fuck she went to.

8.

I order a bottle of Nigori and a spider roll. While I wait for the Sake, I jot down a few thoughts on the project I'm leaning more towards turning into the next book.

Just the fact that I've found myself in this position is insanely frustrating and gut wrenching, yet it's this goddamn indecision about how to proceed forward that's making me the most miserable.

It all feels so overwhelming.

I'm drowning most days anymore.

Thank god the bottle arrives right now.

Where I'm sitting is about ten seats from where Allison and I sat last year. We were in the corner and I remember feeling really bored while I listened to her go on and on about her day at work.

It wasn't that I didn't care at all.

It's just that eighty percent of the shit she ever talked about had to do with this particular job, which just wasn't interesting, and I know it bothered her immensely when I'd make piercing observations comparing a slow death to waking up at seven in the morning five days a week, then commuting to a building where the majority of your waking hours will be spent, just to sit at a desk and do everything your superiors tell you to do (crossing those tasks off on a spreadsheet made just for you) before commuting back home, maybe after a drink or two with your co-workers who apparently say or do some really "hilarious" shit.

The dying continues even though you're not at work anymore because while you prepare dinner, you talk about your job.

And while you eat dinner, you're still talking about your job.

It consumes your existence.

This "whatever" job that means nothing and isn't important.

And it killed her that I refused to acknowledge her "career's" importance.

She was hurt to some degree by my inability to accept that what she did could actually be fulfilling.

When Allison and I first met, *Exit Here* was the only book I had out and it wasn't very successful yet, which meant I had to survive as well. I worked as an assistant property manager for a wine storage company for over a year. And just like she did, I woke up early Monday through Friday and sat in an office and did the things I was assigned to do, which was horribly unsatisfying.

I was never compelled to talk about it over dinner or on the weekends.

In fact, I tried to avoid mentioning it at all costs.

Thing is, that job wasn't an aspiration or a stepping stone to a destination (even though the company had approached me multiple times about their desire for me to move up within the business as they expanded).

What kind of fucking life do I want? I was always thinking.

Like, *This is the mark, the fucking legacy, the way I wanna spend the rest of my years on this place*, which just happen to be the only fucking years you get on this goddamn place.

Allison wanted to be a lawyer once. She'd decided that in college. Once she received her bachelor's degree, she told me her plan had been to apply for law school and start chasing her dream.

But instead of going after it, her super rich best friend's parents bought them tickets to go to Europe and she left, staying there for three months (leaving just a couple of weeks after me and her had begun fucking) and while she was over there, the company she works for now emailed her about an open position they had.

This is what finally prompted her to come home to San Francisco.

We celebrated over dinner the night she was offered the job.

While we were eating, I asked her about law school and she just shrugged.

But by her third glass of wine, suddenly law school wasn't right for her.

There was no guarantee she was going to get in.

Just applying was really expensive. She wasn't

sure she'd be able to do the kind of good things for people that this new job was all about doing.

"I just don't think I have it in me right now," she said. "Not that kind of dedication to really get after it and make it happen."

I nodded and told her I understood.

But I didn't.

I never will.

Me, I decided I wanted to be an author after I started college despite me not knowing at all if my writing was good enough to elevate it from just a passion to a passion with benefits.

Most of the people in my life at that time, including a few instructors at my school and some close friends of mine, they scoffed at me when I told them I'd like to write books for a living.

I ignored them as much as one actually can and began to crib what would become *Exit Here*.

And I worked on it obsessively.

Anytime my mind wandered into the future to see what future me might be up to, the images were always of me sitting alone in a room and typing. Not once do I remember seeing myself at some office wearing slacks and a button up shirt, giving weekly rundowns to my superiors and sitting in a break room talking about my plans for the upcoming weekend.

The process was long and taxing.

It rocked my patience and sharpened my edge.

And then finally, just over a year after I'd signed *Exit Here* with my agent, I received a call from him that Simon & Schuster (the world's third largest publishing house) had made an offer to buy the book. I was fucking ecstatic. To this day, it remains the single happiest moment of my life.

But even though I'd done something so rare and so fucking difficult and done it on my first try, I knew everything was about to get even tougher.

This is art we're talking about. And I wanted art to be my career. I wanted to live off of my writing, which is not only damn near impossible and rare, but the time and the energy and the work that goes into it, like fuck law school and med school and your MBA program, making a living as an artist is and will always be the hardest way to earn a living but it was the only fucking thing I wanted to do.

So after I wrote *Exit Here*, I took that office job just like Allison took hers (except mine paid better, I had better benefits, I got all sorts of perks like free cases of wine, comped meals at neighborhood restaurants, free Giants tickets, and exclusive winery tours anytime I wanted) but unlike Allison, I wanted more out of my life. I wanted the career I'd been dreaming about.

Five months after I'd first pitched the idea of *The Mission* to my agent, not only had the book been written but it'd been sold to Simon & Schuster. Then two months after the release of *The Mission*, after spending one fucking night, just one night a week at my house instead of hers writing the outline for a new book that I'd been kicking around my head for seven years, my agent called me to inform me that Simon & Schuster was offering me a multiple book deal worth nearly six figures.

It was so fucking perfect and so fucking beautiful and the best part about it wasn't the money or the fucking contract perks, it was how I was about to be spending the majority of my time, just all of my goddamn mornings, days, and nights if I wanted to, making art on my own fucking terms.

I'd done what I'd set out to do without ever even entertaining the notion of compromising that goal.

While Allison, this worldly traveler with a 4.0 GPA, the kind of girl who's born with a boyfriend and a golden parachute, watched me not leave for the office every morning, watched me do piles of cocaine off plates in her apartment at nine in the morning, pounding greyhounds and watching Goodfellas, watched me never utter a single fucking sentence for three years that started with the words, "So my boss."

And most of all, she watched me be more productive than anyone she knew as I pounded and cribbed two five hundred plus page books in ten months.

And so there we were in that corner a year ago, me bored despite this flurry of violent images that smashed through my head for a few moments of me beating the piss out of her jerkoff boss who I knew had been trying to fuck her since he'd hired her, and I remember her pausing for a moment as she slid just a tiny bit in her seat so that she was straight in front of me.

She tossed her hair before pulling it back into a bun.

The way she fucking looked in that brief moment, like Audrey Hepburn on the cover of *Vanity Fair* in their May 2013 issue, it left me breathless as I recalled a night a few weeks earlier when we watched one of my favorite movies, *The Woman In The Window*.

During this very subtle moment, I remembered one of the very first things I thought about Allison the day I met her:

She's got this old Hollywood aesthetic and aura about her that's effortless and captivating.

After the movie was over that night, we went for a walk. It was drizzling and she told me she felt like doing something crazy and spontaneous.

I had nothing to offer at that particular moment.
But it didn't matter.
She took me by the hand and we hurried to the MOMA.

She led me straight to this Basquiat piece and as I was studying it, she hiked the back of her dress up then planted her hands against the wall right next to the painting, and I fucked her from behind right there, easily coming in less than two minutes.

Right after I pour my first glass of Sake, I hear a familiar voice from behind me saying, "Well, well, well. A Jason Myers sighting after four in the afternoon. Thought nothing good happened after dark anymore."

Looking over my shoulder, I can't help but smile at the sight of Carlie Adrian walking towards me. As always, she looks fantastic, but like always, it looks like she's either in the middle of a bender or just getting over one, which means she could look even better than she does right now, which is a pretty fucking spectacular quality to have.

"Hey, babe," I say. "Have a seat."

Winking as she runs her fingers across my shoulder, she falls into the seat next to me.

"You look great," I say.

"You ain't looking so bad yourself."

A few jet black streaks run down her dyed red hair. Her bangs are very short and cut evenly across her forehead.

She's wearing a black sleeveless dress with a white collar.

And a pair of black leather fuck me boots cover her legs from the knees down.

Carlie's tattoos color her entire body.

Her and I met the first time during one of the break up portions of the makeup, breakup year Allison and I were engaged in.

It was about a month before we finally and permanently severed ourselves from each other.

The reason for our particular split during that period was because Allison refused to answer a question I had about a picture one of my friends had seen of her on Facebook.

In the photo, Allison had stripped down to just her bra and underwear and was sitting in between two dudes in a hot tub.

It was posted on the same night of the day that Allison cancelled our dinner plans because she wasn't feeling well.

Two days went by before I heard from her again.

She had no idea I'd seen the photo.

When we finally saw each other again, I suggested we go out for a couple of drinks and she told me she wanted to go to this lame wine bar on Divisadero called Vinyl.

I hate that place for a number of reasons.

The main one being the ridiculously arrogant motherfucker who I think manages it.

Allison and I had gone there a handful of times before and that chubby d-bag was always hitting on her in front of me by making condescending remarks towards me.

That night, after I confronted her about the photo and she denied its existence and we got into a fairly explosive argument before I backed off, that dude slipped her his number on a napkin while I was in the bathroom.

But the napkin fell out of her purse and I saw it.

Allison told me not to make a big deal out of it, which I didn't.

Instead, I politely called him over to us and asked him if he'd like to have a word with me outside. His face turned red and he stuttered like a bitch as he tried to manufacture a bit of bullshit to excuse his behavior.

But I wasn't buying it.

So to make amends, the dude poured us each a glass of Pinot Noir on the house.

I laughed at him.

And then I lit a cigarette at the bar, took two drags, then put it out in my wine and walked away, leaving Allison just for him.

The next night, I was on my way to a radio interview to talk about this short story I'd written, The Wax Pimp, *and I stopped by the Latin American Club for a margarita and there was the young and gorgeous and sexy, Carlie.*

She was wearing a blue sundress, and swaying all by herself in the middle of the floor along with that Mickey and Sylvia song, "Love Is Strange".

I couldn't look away from her.

I didn't wanna blink.

I had to meet this girl.

I had to know who she was.

Once the song ended, she strolled over to a table occupied by three girls.

Fucking dykes.

Goddamnit!

This was the first thought that slammed through my head.

Like, for sure two of them were.

The real chubby two with the boy haircuts.

One wearing trousers and the other wearing suspenders and a bow tie.

The third girl was also a babe but she didn't have nothing on my tiny dancer in the blue dress.

Common sense told me these girls were together.

And then I watched the other pretty one kiss the gross one in suspenders and I knew I had my work cut out for me.

Plus, I was vaguely pissed off about the two fatties being capable enough to pull this kind of tail.

Perhaps it's something in the genetic disposition of queers, but it's always bothered me to see thin, glowing, gorgeous lesbians with a gnar-pig girlfriend.

Just like it bothers me whenever I see beautiful women with mouth breathing man slobs.

It just happens way more in dyke land.

I had to be at the interview in less than thirty minutes, but at that point I was willing to blow it off in order to meet this girl.

Thank God she was a smoker.

Attempting to mask my eagerness to make her acquaintance, I waited a whole thirty seconds or so to follow her outside after she dug a pack of smokes out of her purse and exited the bar.

What happened next though, it surprised me.

As I was about to light my grit, she approached me and I got so nervous that I lit my cigarette backwards.

"First time," she said.

"No," I said back. "I'm not sure what that was."

She laughed. "You looked distracted."

"Did I?"

She nodded and went, "Here, love," and then took the lit cigarette from between her lips, slid it between mine, and lit a new one for herself. "I wouldn't want you to waste another one."

"I appreciate that."

"I'm Carlie," she said.

"Jason."

"So what's up?" she said.

"What do you mean?"

"Don't do that," she said, frowning.

"What are you talking about?"

"I was watching you watching me," she went.

"And now you're out here right after I walk out here."

I blushed.

And I said, "So you're the only one who can smoke when they feel like it?"

"Forget it," she said, rolling her eyes.

"Wait," I said as she turned away. "Why are you upset?"

"I'm not," she said.

"What's with the attitude then?"

"All you've done since you got here is watch me. Since you walked in, your whole world has been me and wondering how I fit in with that table of girls in there."

I didn't say anything.

And she went, "I smoke maybe four cigarettes a month, Jason."

"What's your point?"

I remember her eyes getting so big I thought they were going to pop out of her face.

And Carlie went, "If you're just fucking with me right now, man. Just stop. We're wasting time."

After she said that, she looked over her shoulder, trying to peer into the bar as best as she could.

"Is there something you think I should be saying to you right now?" I asked her.

She looked utterly disappointed. "I guess not. I mean, unless there's something you wanted to say to me but thought you couldn't inside because of who I'm with."

"I think you're fucking gorgeous," I finally blurted out. "I also think you're a lesbian. But not a real one."

Laughter exploded from her mouth and she said, "What do you know about lesbians?"

"Not much," I told her. "What I meant though was that I think you're probably way more into dudes than whatever is sitting at that fucking table right now."

"Hey-" she started.

But I cut her off. And I said, "It fucking sucks to get ruined by someone you really fucking believed cherished you and respected you. And every time it happens to me, I start doing enough cocaine to kill Nikki Sixx again. I start drinking so much tequila, I swear it's what sprays out of my dick when I piss. And like ninety percent of my time involves listening to Wu-Tang records and memorizing ODB interviews."

She looked so confused. "What's your point?"

"I don't start sucking dicks or slamming fat chicks because some cunt broke my heart."

Carlie didn't say anything. She didn't have to. She was smiling and her hand was wrapped around my arm.

And I went, "Anyway, the other thing I do is I try to find someone even more beautiful and more sexy and way more fun."

"Is that right?"

"It is. But why take my word for it?"

"Jesus," she said, looking away from me and squeezing her forehead.

I checked the time on my phone. The interview was in fifteen minutes and I still needed to stop at a liquor store and pick up supplies.

"I have to go," I told Carlie.

"Right this second?"

"Yeah. Right this second."

I told her what I was doing and where I had to go and that she should find a computer somewhere or a radio and listen to the broadcast.

"You do not want to miss this," I said. "My radio interviews are fucking legendary."

She said she'd try which meant she would definitely not be listening, which was fine.

This is San Francisco.

This is 2014.

All the technology and social media created to keep us more connected, to bring us closer together, has really just made it more possible to disengage, flake, and outright lie.

So I asked her for her phone number next.

And she said, "No."

"Okay."

"I'm sorry," she said.

"Don't be."

"It was really nice talking to you, Jason."

"At least you remembered my name," I told her.

I watched her walk back inside the bar and imagined she was going to kiss that other ugly, man looking dyke, and I imagined she'd play fake queer for a few more months until the rest of the bitter taste left from the last dude she loved who didn't love her the same way back was finally gone from her sweet, sweet mouth.

Twenty minutes after she walked away from me though, during the first commercial break of the interview, there was this super loud pounding on the door of the tiny studio where we were broadcasting from.

Trevor, the guy interviewing me, he walked out of the room we were in and answered it. My fucking heart skipped about ten beats. Standing in the doorway with a twelve pack of Corona, a lime, a bottle of tequila, and a huge fucking smile was Carlie.

I almost fell out of my chair.

While Trevor and I settled back in to begin the next segment (which was ten minutes straight of us talking about the specifics of how one would go about creating the certain areas needed to have intercourse with a wax figure), Carlie sliced the lime, she poured three shots, and she made six lines of cocaine on the cover of The Replacements Let It Be *record which I took a special liking to since that's what Michael did in* Exit Here *the first time him and Travis hung out after Travis returned home.*

Needless to say, it was like, Fuck Allison.

That stupid fucking whore.

And it was like, 'Sup Carlie. And she hung out for the whole interview which really fucking impressed her. How I had four fucking novels published, sitting on shelves in bookstores worldwide, with a fifth one on the way. She was even more impressed by me not having said anything about the books to her while we were at the Latin American Club (when I mentioned the radio interview, I told her it was because of a project I'd done a couple years ago and that was it).

It was just so great to have her there.

We integrated her into the discussion and asked her to name the wax celebrities she'd most like to fuck. She talked about being kidnapped once in Reno and spending nine hours in a car trunk before escaping in

Carson City, stealing a gun from the back of a pick-up truck, then finding her captors and tying them up and taking off with their duffel bag filled with five thousand dollars cash, a hundred Fossil watches, like twenty Barack Obama bobble heads, a Lady Gaga chia pet, and four Air Supply cassette tapes.

During every commercial break, the three of us danced. And during the final segment, she took my hand and placed it on the inside of her thigh, then let me do the rest.

As I explained the process of writing Blazed (live on the fucking air), and the radical evolvement both the book and I went through (Blazed will be my masterpiece even though it didn't start out like it would be), I was also explaining (with my fingers) to Carlie, the possibilities of pleasure she had to look forward to in the future with me by ditching that tired, boring dyke act that so many girls I know fucking turn to and honestly believe makes them like unique and special which it doesn't at all. In fact, it does the opposite. It reveals to the world that they don't know how to be happy, that they don't know themselves that well, and that they've decided not to take a good look at themselves and accept any of the responsibility for the event or series of events that led them to thinking that dating girls or fucking girls was an honest solution to absolving the misery of their continued relationship failures with men.

By the time the segment ended, Carlie was still shaking from her second orgasm and my fingers were a dripping mess. Trevor, who never knew that was happening (he was fucking shocked when I told him a few weeks later when I ran into him at the Nick Cave and the Bad Seeds show), he left the room to piss, and I licked my fingers clean and Carlie made three more lines and while she did, she brought up a couple parts of the story I'd told about the writing of this book and what she thought of it which sorta blew me away. She'd listened to every word I'd said.

Turns out, that was pretty much the last time she listened to really anything I was ever saying.

9.

"Who was that girl with you in L.A.?" Carlie asks me now after I pour another glass of Sake and offer her some.

She grabs the bottle and takes a swig from it. I start laughing.

"So..." she presses.

"No one," I say. "Just a girl."

"Didn't look like just a girl," she goes.

"Why do you fucking care, Carlie? Get off my fucking page."

"You're such a jerk," she says. "You always have been. All these people think you're this real sweetheart. They think you're this nice, standup guy, but it's bullshit and you know it too and you've been laughing about it since your first book took off. Just laughing at everyone you've been fooling."

An image of me grabbing Carlie's hair, yanking her into the bathroom, and bending her over the sink smashes through my head.

And I almost just do it. Like for real. My right hand even gets in place to make a clean grab and pull. This should be happening and I should be fucking Carlie in thirty seconds and there's a significant part of me that knows she's expecting me to at least propose some sorta sexual rendezvous.

Instead though, I allow my hand to relax, and I say, "You do a lot of things very well, doll. But the one thing you've never done anything but fail at is masking your envy and your jealousy and your absolute inability to accept even the slightest responsibility for this treadmill your life has been running on these last coupla years."

She scowls before pounding the rest of the Sake.

Me, I spin around to see who she happens to be here with.

"Go on," she snaps, when I turn back to her.

Grinning, I go, "What?"

"So I'm with Lauren again," she says. "Get it over with, Jason. Go on. Tell me what you really think about me now."

"Nothing," I say. "I don't give a shit at all that you're back with that fat fucking lesbian pastry chef who used to lock you in her closet and make you listen to Smash Mouth records until you'd come clean about where and who you'd been with."

"That only happened once, Jason. Jesus Christ. One time."

"It's still one of the best fucking stories I've ever heard, babe. That's one thing I'll always love about you, Carlie. Your stories. You know how to tell a great fucking story. There ain't a boring bone in that sweet, sweet body of yours."

I slide my hand over her thigh after I say this.

And then I go, "Did I ever tell you I thought about doing that to Allison once?"

Carlie removes my hand now. "Fuck that bitch."

"Sure," I say. "But there was this one time near the end, like the real, real end of me and her and I hadn't heard a word from her in three days aside from her forwarding me this email from Groupon for like thirty percent off at the oyster place in the Ferry Building, and when we did see each other next, I remembered that story and actually thought about doing something similar. I even went out and bought a fucking Bush CD but then realized later on that she fucking loved Bush and once spent four fucking hours searching the internet for a video of them singing "Glycerine" in a rainstorm. That tasteless fucking slut."

Carlie laughs hard now and gasps, "Damn you."

"Go on."

"I miss you sometimes, Jason. A lot."

"We weren't very good together, Carlie."

"How can you say that?" she snaps. "We were great when you were all the way in, Jason. When you were actually there. But you never were for more than a night or two at a time."

She says, "That first week we had together, like fuck. It's still the best week I've ever had with another person. I'd only been fucking girls for five years before I met you. And then you fucked me the second night we saw each other. You fucked me for like seven hours and I'd never been fucked liked that in my life. I wanted you so badly. I was ready to give up everything, Jason, and then you just fucking disappeared. I didn't talk to you for almost two months. You disappeared the night after we did all the Molly and I rode you for like an hour and you demanded me to keep punching you in the face and right before you came, you told me you loved me."

My appetite disappears immediately after she says this last part and I wave the waitress over and order another bottle of Sake and tell Carlie, "Just because someone tells you they love you doesn't mean that you belong with that person."

She sighs, shaking her head slowly. "I know."

"Do you?" I snap.

"I do now," she says.

"I'm not even sorry about any of that either," I tell her. "And I never will be."

I finish my glass and tap my fingers against the bar.

"What do you want?" she asks me.

I make a face and go, "That's not even a real question."

"Yes it is," she says.

"Okay, fine. It's a loaded fucking question then."

"You don't even know, do you?"

"Carlie," I say. "What does it matter to you?"

"Because I fucking care. I'm gorgeous, I'm smart, I'm fun, I love your books, and I was loyal to you."

The new bottle of Sake arrives and I go, "What about that one time when I gave you three hundred dollars to go get coke and you didn't come back for like twelve hours and then I found out that you were at your dealer's crib playing Xbox with two strippers from the Crazy Horse and buying Motley Crue tickets with the money."

Her face turns white.

Me, I pour another glass, and go, "Forgot about that didn't you?"

"So we're gonna play gotcha now."

"I got you. I mean, it's awesome, what you were doing, but still, babe."

"You were gone when I finally did come back, Jason. You went to Allison's, turned your phone off for a week and posted on Facebook that you got robbed and they took your phone."

"I did get robbed."

"No you did not!"

"I did too. I got robbed before we ever met, Carlie. Robbed of the rest of my life that was going to be perfect and beautiful. Me and her and our house in Montana."

"You told me you two made that pact on Molly."

"It was still a pact, Carlie."

"What do you want?" she asks again.

This time, I pick the bottle up and go, "Something beautiful, Carlie. Something young and beautiful and smarter than me. A girl who hasn't been touched by this life we live. A happy girl. A girl who doesn't need to pound a bottle of champagne and a half gram of coke to actually enjoy being awake. It was like that at the beginning with Allison, ya know."

"What happened?"

"I happened."

"Enough said," she goes.

"I mean last week, I went to the movies and had to leave halfway through it."

"Why?"

"Because I ran out of blast."

"Jesus Christ."

"Plus this lady sitting behind me, she actually said *Chinatown* was overrated. That cunt. She actually said that the greatest movie ever made was overrated so then I turn around and I see her and she's wearing a baggy hooded sweatshirt that says Chico State on it and over half the bucket of popcorn on her lap was gone. And the fucking previews hadn't even started yet. I was so upset that I stayed in my room for an entire day."

"Are you depressed?"

"What kind of question is that?"

"It's just a question," she says.

Leaning forward as I slide my hand through my hair and down my face, I go, "Honestly, babe?"

"Yes."

"I'm scared, Carlie."

"Of what?"

"This," I say, holding my arms out. "I'm scared of what's happening to this city. I'm scared cos my writing career is on life support and I've got nothing left from it. I'm broke. I don't see any of my old friends anymore. I'm terrified of having to even think about getting anything even remotely close to a "real" job again. I'm scared of getting old and being alone. I'm starting to lose my fucking hair."

"I see that."

"Fuck you."

"Go on."

"I was at a party a coupla weeks ago and actually started a story with, 'Back when I was a kid and just moved here,' in a room full of young, like twenty-one year old's and none of them listened to another word of my story and then I let some pretty, young blonde haired girl who flirted hard with me for a minute take my sack of blast to the bathroom with her, then I had to spend twenty minutes looking for her, and when I found her she handed it back to me and the fucking thing was empty, and I didn't even say anything about it and she called me Josh."

"Ouch," Carlie hisses. "You killed her didn't you?"

"Thought about it. But like five years ago, I woulda been in the girl's bathroom already doing the white bitch, not the girl, the coke I mean, and when I would've been ready to leave the party, I would've put my arm around her, told her we were going to my crib, and pulled her into the cab with me. And when we got back to my place, if the Black Angels were the only band I wanted to listen to the rest of the night..."

"Go on."

I say, "Then the Black Angels woulda been the only band we listened to. And if I wanted her to suck my dick while I typed a chapter, she woulda sucked my dick while I typed a chapter."

"I did that for you, Jason."

"No you didn't."

"Yes, I did. I listened to the Black Angels with you one night and just them."

"Oh. I meant the last thing."

"I'd do that for you tonight," she says. "If you wanted me to."

"I've been writing a lot of poetry lately."

"Let me come over later. I'll suck your dick while you read the poetry."

"Carlie," I start.

But she cuts me off.

And she goes, "What the fuck do you want?"

"Cocaine. Right now. Do you have any?"

She looks back at the table her girlfriend and homies are sitting at.

"You've changed," I say.

"Bullshit. Meet me in the bathroom in five minutes."

"Yeah?"

"Yes."

Carlie gets up and she walks over to her girlfriend and they talk for a minute while my first roll gets set in front of me.

I pick up my first piece with a pair of chopsticks. It's so fucking delicious too. And then Carlie walks past me, winking, and heads down the hallway for the ladies room.

Me, I finish the Sake, then I lay a hundred dollar bill on the bar.

Whatever this is, I ain't going back to that.

So instead of going to the bathroom, I stand up and I leave Tokyo-A-Go-Go and hail a cab.

"The Knockout please," I say. "Mission and 30th."

Then I shut my phone off because I don't wanna read about how awful I really am because Carlie can cut some serious fucking glass with her texts.

If anyone should be a writer, it should be her. Even when she's loaded, that bitch doesn't waste a single fucking word.

10.

The Knockout.

I ain't been here in at least two years.

The show I saw that night was pretty epic, I think. It was 400 Blows, The Fleshies, and The Grannies.

I even blacked out, which happens maybe once a year, if that. And here's the final thing I remember: this babe with short black hair, tattoos, wearing a sleeveless These Arms Are Snakes t-shirt picks my beer up, takes a drink from it, then sits down next to me, and says, "*I would fucking break you.*"

"*What the fuck kind of thing is that to say to someone?*" I snapped back.

"*I'm going to fucking break you tonight. Is that a better fucking thing to say someone?*" she ripped, grinning from ear to ear.

I loved where this was going way too much but I didn't want it to go there so I called Allison and she showed up in a cab to take me to her place (which I don't remember at all). The next morning though, she was super upset with me, and when I asked her why, she said that I'd called her an office slave and a prostitute (she lived rent free at her boyfriend's house for five years and was still living there when I began stabbing her vag) and that I threw out all this fish she'd bought at Trader Joe's earlier that day for this really nice dinner she wanted to cook for us.

"*Did I say why I was throwing it out?*" I asked her, as I smashed the remainder of the blow I found in my wallet right up my nose after laughing for like twenty minutes because I thought I'd seen all this drool coming out of Julia Child's mouth on TV.

"*You were mad that I'd bought the fish. That I'd paid for it. Instead of giving me money for it, you threw it out and told me that you were the man of the house, the provider, and then you asked me for twenty dollars to go get ice cream, cigarettes, The New York Times, and champagne at the store.*"

"*Sorry,*" I told her. "*Like, my intentions were pretty okay though.*"

"*You wanted to put a gram of cocaine in my roommate's suitcase, Jason. So that when she went to the airport this morning, she'd get busted for it.*"

"*She tried to set you up on a date with that friend of hers who wears baggy jeans and plays hacky sack. Trust me, babe. I was letting her off easy.*"

Allison threw her arms in the air and stormed out of the house without telling me where she was going. Four hours later, she finally came back as I was putting the finishing touches on the wonderful dinner I decided to make for her because of what I'd done.

We started with my sweet potato fries and this amazing artichoke salad.

Then moved on to my three layer jalepeno mac 'n cheese dish.

And ended with my brownie and ice cream dessert.

There were also three bottles of eighty dollar Pinot Noir that one of my best friends, who happens to be a major player in the wine industry up north in Napa and Sonoma, dropped off. And thirty year aged bourbon, which hadn't been opened yet, and was given to me by my wonderful agent two years earlier while I was in New York.

Back to the Knockout.

It's fucking sold out and the door guy refuses to play ball with me so I text the bar manager, this dude Ricky, and he comes out, and we smoke a cigarette, and then he walks me in and hands me six drink tickets.

Asphyxiated is setting up right now. Even though the Knockout is a pain in the ass to get to because it's so deep in the Mission, I fall head over heels back in love with it immediately.

The Stooges *Raw Power* is blasting from the house speakers. Pretty girls and boys in leather jackets, jean jackets, tight jeans, ripped stockings, with amazing haircuts and boots and shoes fill every fucking inch of this place.

And I'm just smiling.

My whole stupid face, just a smear of happy.

Because it's the same fucking place it's always been to me. The first show I saw here was 400 Blows, Nigel Peppercock, and the Knights Of The New Crusade way back in 2002. And unlike the lower Mission that stretches from 13th to 25th, this area has yet to go through the same radical gentrification of its significant other.

This is something to celebrate, I guess.

Me on the prowl for cocaine and pussy at one of the last establishments still standing and unchanged. Still filled with the reality and the nostalgia and the style and the glory of the Mission from 2002-2009.

At the bar, I order a shot of tequila and a Pacifico. Then I turn my phone back on which terrifies me because of how I left Tokyo-A-Go-Go. I mean, it really fucking shakes me. Like, I'd rather be fetching Darius Rucker coffee on the set of *Sesame Street* than feel my phone vibrate a million times from the million hate filled, horrific, and violent texts that I'm sure Carlie's already sent.

But I don't see Ryan anywhere and I want him to know I'm here. When the bartender sets my drinks down in front of me, she goes, "I know you."

"Great."

"Seriously," she goes. "Your band played here a couple of years ago."

"Yes we did," I snort. "Oh wow."

"Wow what?"

"We were sort of a nightmare that night. A total shitshow."

She shrugs and shakes her head. "It was fun, man."

"We sounded like shit though which was a bummer. The fucking sound guy refused to tweak anything we were asking him to during the set. And I'm pretty sure we didn't play a single one of our songs right. I think we left a verse or two out of every one. It was pretty ridiculous."

"No," she goes. "You guys were totally ridiculous but it worked."

"No it didn't."

"For me it did. I mean, I didn't know your band before that night so I didn't know any of the songs but who the fuck cares? You guys were fun to watch. You actually put on a show. And I thought some of the songs ripped pretty tough."

I pour the shot down my throat, then suck on the lime it came with, and then my phone just starts going off. I glance at it quickly and see that there are twenty-seven texts from Carlie and four voicemails.

I take a minute and delete all of it without reading a single word or listening to a single second, before saying, "Are you fucking with me right now?"

"No." she laughs. "I had a blast watching you dudes up there in your white jeans, and the fake blood, you running through that lame fucking crowd of "coolsters" who refused to stand any closer than like ten feet from the stage. And then it was you, I think, who started throwing beers from your cooler into the crowd and then told them to throw it and spray back on you."

"That was me."

"It was real, ya know. Like I knew you guys were having a fucking blast playing."

Her telling me this should be making me feel better about tonight and the night we played here but it's not and that's because I don't see Ryan anywhere which is really starting to crease me and make me hate the faces of everyone in this stupid place.

"You okay?" she asks me when I still haven't responded to what she said about us being "real" that night.

Rolling my eyes, I go, "We were having fun. That's all. Fun was always our fucking thing. We'd play the show but we'd also put on a show. Some people loved the fuck out of what we were doing and a lot of people hated our guts. We never cared too much either way. I never felt bad if anyone hated our music or had a shitty time. The whole time we were together as a band, we never pretended that we were anything other than what we were. Not once. It's why I always said, 'Welcome to the shitshow' right before we'd rip into our first song."

She starts laughing and goes, "I actually think I remember you saying that."

"Damn, girl," I say. "I don't even know what to say to all of this."

"Nothing," she goes, winking. "This first rounds on me."

"Thanks," I tell her, pulling my drink tickets out. "But Ricky gave me these."

"Save 'em," she says. "These are on me. Have fun, love."

Turning from the bar now, part of me wonders if that was a really cool thing that just happened while another part of me wonders if that bitch needs to get a new job. Could be she's been working here too long if she remembered Wounded Bloody Hole playing here and thought that was fun and thought we were having fun.

I was fucking miserable during that set despite spending the entire day of the show at the Phoenix Hotel fucking this beautiful blonde from Los Angeles (Allison and I were on another like two week separation) and drinking some kind of insane amount of champagne by the pool.

No one in the band was able to score any blast that night either.

It was the strangest fucking thing too.

If Wounded Bloody Hole was any kind of band, we were a cocaine band first, a cocaine band second, and a curserap/cocaine band third.

But for whatever reason, we got iced on that shit that night which meant I was totally doomed and I knew it.

I remember sitting at the bar about five minutes before we were supposed to start ripping, and I turned to Farah (the super babe from Los Angeles I was slaying at the Phoenix who'd just walked in like a minute earlier and for whatever reason, was dressed like she was attending a "Businesswomen In Power" conference) and said, "I'm thinking about splitting."

"Right now, Jason?"

I nodded, and went, "Yes. Preferably right now."

"What's wrong?"

"I can't do this without snorting the rails of glory first."

She made a face and wildly shook her head. "I don't know what that fucking means, dude. Why do you want to leave your show without playing it?"

"There's no cocaine here."

"Oh, fuck that," she said. "You're so ridiculous. What are you talking about?"

"Can I have your room key?"

"No."

"Farah," I said. "I don't wanna play."

The second after I said that too, my phone buzzed. It was a text from my bass player.

"See," I said, then held it up for her to read.

The text said: Hey, man. We've prolly got two minutes to grab any of the shit we brought and bail. I can barely stand and I've been trying to text you that for a half an hour.

"Just play," Farah snapped. "One of the reasons I came to San Francisco was to see your band, Jason."

"Really?" I went. "You did this just to see my band?"

She shrugged and went, "Sure. I'm here, right?"

"Why are you dressed like that?" I asked.

Another text from my bass player showed up and that one said, The sound guy just said we have to go on. Are you going to sing?

I looked at Farah and went, "My mom wears suits like those."

But before she could start yelling at me, I heard our drummer starting to fuck around on stage. When I stood up, I almost fell over but Farah helped me get to the other end of the bar and the bartender handed me a small cooler filled with cans of Olympia.

When I stepped onto the stage, my bass player was dousing himself with fake blood. Our drummer looked pale and was sweating. I'd seen him pounding a bottle of Kraken rum in his friend's pick-up truck when I was getting out of the cab in front of the Knockout.

You know how someone looks like they're wishing for death when they've gotten seafood poisoning, this dude's glossed over, empty eyes were casing the joint for the grim reaper.

Grabbing the microphone, I said the thing I always say and we proceeded to play the worst show of our short lived careers as members of Bloody Wounded Hole.

It was great.

I even got threatened halfway through the set by some fat dude in the band playing after us and then in between "Stiff Dick Mental" and our hit, "Period Ballin" someone yelled that we sucked and I said, "Yeah. But we suck the best."

Immediately after we were done playing, I walked off the stage, grabbed Farah, and we jumped into a cab and went straight back to the Phoenix and opened a bottle of Stoli.

I ended up staying there with her for two more days and like four days later my third novel, Dead End *was released worldwide.*

Fast-forward three years now and here I am again at the Knockout in desperate need of cocaine except, this time, I'm all alone. I have no band, no girl (not even one I can break up and make up with), I haven't seen anyone that I know yet except Ricky but me and him just know each other from running into one another while we're scoring shit at Ryan's crib, and my next book coming out could be my last book and I have no plan B.

For the first time in my life, I'm terrified about my future and its trajectory (or lack thereof) and the fact that I'm really out of shape and I'm beginning to lose my hair.

Anxiety covers me like wet fur.

That whole never talk to strangers shit my mom used to tell me as a child, well, it's one of the only pieces of advice I've ever truly lived by and taken all the way to heart.

And so this is how it is tonight:

Isolated.

Nervous.

Missing Allison.

Missing Natasha and that sweet, shaved, young pussy of hers. And missing the chunks of white my bronze house key should be covered with by now.

Pushing myself towards the stage, I can't take my eyes off the insanely pretty girl from Asphyxiated. I wish I had the guts to approach her but even if I did, I'm pretty positive I'd be one out of a hundred other dudes she has to deal with every time her band plays which has to get really old and really annoying like really fast.

Plus, a girl that pretty and talented and stylish, girls like that are born with fucking boyfriends.

As The Stooges fade into the MC5, I finish my beer and head outside for a cigarette.

Still nothing from Ryan.

Walking about twenty feet from the Knockout entrance, I lean against the window of this shop and light my grit.

Inhale. Exhale.

"Titty Coke Montana!" I hear someone yell, and look to my left.

"Holy shit!" I snort back. "Keith fucking Nightmare! Yes!"

"Get the fuck over here!" he yells. "And give your daddy a big 'ole huggy hug!"

Me and Keith, we go way back to my beginning in this city. Dude's like six feet tall. Has long, curly black hair. He's all tatted up. And we've prolly found ourselves backing each other up in at least thirty fistfights throughout the years.

Anymore though, we rarely see each other. He's in Oakland now. He's in the horticulture business and doing pretty fucking well for himself. Last I heard, he had a boat and him and Sean Penn played laser tag for two and half days straight in the Marin woods.

I roll over to him and we fist bump and hug and he snatches the smoke from between my lips and takes a couple of drags before flicking it into the street.

"Shit'll kill you," he snaps.

"Shit costs me money too," I snap back.

"So what's the deal?" he goes. "They won't let me in."

"Sold out."

"Fuck that," he goes. "Five years ago, me and you coulda cut the line and walked right in without paying."

"I know. But it ain't the same, homie. This place is the same but we ain't running nothing no more."

"Tell me about it. I'm more successful than I've ever been at any point in my life. I've got a Benz, a warehouse in Oakland, a collection of fur coats, and I really do know James Spader now, but seven years ago, when me and you were living in the Tenderloin buying forties with change and robbing people sometimes to pay our rent, there wasn't a party or a club or a bar we paid to get into or ever waited in line to get into."

"I remember, man. This city has changed."

"It has," he says. "But so have we."

"You think?"

"Duh, faggot. Me and you and all those fools we came up with in the city, we ain't going out every night anymore. We ain't hitting every after party or just pulling babes we laid eyes on five seconds earlier into cabs with us. We ain't doing cocaine with the owners of these places till eight a.m. anymore."

"That's for sure."

"We chose to be successful, motherfucker. That's why dating these hot young bitches who just moved here sucks. They wanna do all the shit we've already done like every night. The guest list is the most important thing in their lives still."

"Oh, the guest list days," I say, then light another grit. "Come with me," I say.

Me and Keith, we walk into this tiny alley half a block down and I ask him if he has any coke.

He doesn't.

He's here looking for Ryan too.

"He's not in there," I tell him. "But I can get you in. That dude Ricky manages this place now."

"Tight Black Hole Ricky?" Keith goes.

"Yeah."

Keith starts laughing and says, "The last time I kicked it with that fucking pilgrim twat was at your place on Van Ness."

It takes me a second before this vague image of *me waking up and seeing this naked girl lying on the couch in our hallway with a bottle of Royal Gate Vodka in her hand, laughing, smashes through my head.*

She was hot, too.

And then I remember hearing people giggling and I looked to the left of my bed and saw Ricky and Keith free basing crystal meth off a piece of broken light bulb. Both of them were naked too, and The Shins were playing from

*somewhere, and they were taking turns hitting the glass
and then walking to the couch and fucking this girl for a
few minutes then walking back into my room and high-
fiving and giggling some more.*

*Then I passed out and when I woke up, my place
was fucking spotless, just so damn clean, and there was a
half gram taped to my desk with a note that said:* Thanks
for letting us have that last night. She wanted to fuck you
but you passed out and then she said she'd never had a
threesome and asked us to play ball. You're the best. And
this coke's for you.

"Damn," I go.

"Crazy shit, man," says Keith.

"And you haven't seen Ricky since?"

"Not that I remember."

"Come on then," I go. "I'll call him right now and
get you in."

"Sweet, brah."

11.

So we spend the next forty-five minutes watching Asphyxiated destroy. And it's one of the best sets I've seen in awhile.

"I guess there is life after the Thee Oh Sees," Keith says.

"There's a coupla bands for sure. These guys. Vicious Lips. Lamborghini Dreams."

Pause.

I devour the rest of my Pacifico.

"Terry Malts," says Keith. "And the Coo Coo Birds."

"Totally," I say. "I should buy a shirt."

"You should ask that girl out," he says.

"Like she hasn't been asked out ten times already tonight," I say back.

When the set's over, I make my way to the merch table and grab a record and a shirt but before I can grab either, I get a text from Ryan that says he's at Lucky 13 now.

Jesus Christ, I'm thinking.

I need a new guy.

I should've bought like three more grams while I was in L.A.

I feel like a fucking amateur right now.

Like some asshole twenty-three year old kid who knows he's gonna need the power powder before he goes out for the night but doesn't get it and then ends up spending way more money in cab fares, ATM charges, and bar covers than he would've if he'd just taken care of business ahead of time.

But whatever.

As I'm turning to walk away from the merch area, I see the girl from Asphyxiated and she sees me and I smile and wink and she does the same but this is as far it'll ever go and that's okay.

Something about her and what she does, how she commands that stage and how sweet and nice she probably is and how stuck and hopeless and old I've become, I don't deserve that kind of awesomeness.

Coexisting with an even kind of well-adjusted, sorta put together girl is something that will never work for me.

Who the fuck wants that or to be around that?

I'll lose interest cos I won't care about whatever plans she has about moving up in whatever world she's found herself confined to fifty hours a week.

I won't actually ever care about what she does during the day if she's not making and creating stuff that has the potential to enhance the life of someone else.

I'll lose interest because I'll feel guilty for not feeling guilty for not at all wanting to change the way I live.

I'm only good with the true messes and the psychopaths.

It's always been this way.

Those beautiful, seemingly ageless, ambitious but directionless ones.

The gorgeous ones who wanna blow off life for a week or so and actually have the guts to do it and then join me at my apartment to drink endless bottles of champagne and whiskey while we lay around in our underwear and debate cinema and literature and Guns N' Roses and the Chuck Mosley era of Faith No More.

The gorgeous ones whose only use for a mirror is the one they're using to blast cocaine off of. The curious ones who wanna be read to then tell me everything I write is amazing before asking me to pass them the mirror again.

I'm here for the ones in search of comfort for their broken souls.

I am their diary.

Their words are the pen.

And I am the quiet pages they use to say all the fucked up things on their minds that nobody else wants to hear at four in the morning.

This is who I'm here for.

The beautiful, young, and sensitive messes who haven't figured out yet how to turn that mess into a success.

The way I did once.

Like some weird magic shit.
My greatest achievement so far.

12.

I find Keith again at the bar and ask him if he got Ryan's text.

He did but he says he's not going. That it's not worth it anymore.

He goes, "My guy in Oakland has better shit and he's taking calls now so I'm heading back there."

"Fuck that," I say.

"You should come, man."

"That sounds like a terribly great idea. But if I go, I know I won't come back to SF anytime soon. I'll prolly end up living over there."

"You should've done that a long time ago, my man. Before the Google monster got y'all."

"Let's do one more shot," I say.

"For sure."

I wave the same bartender from earlier back over and order two more shots of tequila.

We down them and then Keith Nightmare, he takes off and I know it's gonna be another coupla years before I see him next.

But it's whatever and shit.

I've heard he still haunts Pop's every now and then still. Showing up with a grip of bullets full of coke and finger banging all the pretty tattooed girls in the bar's photo booth.

An image which actually makes me extremely happy.

Back outside now.

I light a cigarette while attempting to hail a cab.

I get a text from Allison that says: *I'm sorry about what I sent you earlier. This is hard, Jason. I miss you. I miss us. I love my boyfriend, but he isn't you. He's not as cool as you or funny as you and doesn't know everyone like you. I just want to laugh every fucking morning again and want to go to cool shows with you and listen to you read to me at night. I'm so pathetic. I know this. But I fucking miss you so much.*

I delete this text immediately. I have to. Otherwise, I'll find myself reading it a thousand fucking times at three in the morning when I'm alone and shitfaced.

And I don't trust myself at that moment enough and in that state to not send her a text about how much I miss her and that we should get back together because we were so great.

We weren't.

Everything about my life except her was so fucking radical and awesome.

That's what I'm really missing.

Not her.

So fuck my nostalgia.

And fuck my stupid phone.

And fuck my shitty bank accounts, my shitty last two books, and my shitty, empty, pointless yearning for "getting my old life back."

It's time to start a new one.

I just have no goddamn idea how to do that.

Hopefully the blast can help.

It's past eleven now and I haven't even thought about the Tiger Kill.

One of the most important places to my life in San Francisco won't exist in three hours and I haven't even attempted to say goodbye to it.

"Jason Myers," I hear, right as I've taken the final drag of my smoke.

I look up and I see Delilah Kaitlyn Lee crossing the street by herself.

Of all the people in my life I'd love to see coming towards me right now, she's the one I'd choose if I had a choice.

A true southern belle from Savannah, Georgia that I kinda dated for a couple of weeks in November.

Delilah is twenty-seven. She's lived in San Francisco for three years. She was once a piercer and tattoo artist in Atlanta but now she owns her own screen printing company and is also getting ready to launch her own record label, Southern Belle Records.

Delilah is so pretty. She's like 5'7 and skinny as a pole. She's got this wavy, dark brown hair that flows down to the middle of her back. These big, round, blue eyes.

Both her arms are sleeved. In fact, I think the work she's gotten on herself is better than any other work I've seen during my entire time in San Francisco. And all of it was done in Japan and Paris between the ages of eighteen and twenty. In fact, she did her apprenticeship in Japan and speaks fluent Japanese and French.

One other thing about Delilah too is that she hates that fucking song, "Hey There Delilah". But she hates it for more than the name thing. She thinks the lyrics are bullshit and that the name of the band who wrote the song is one of the worst band names ever (which I think is pretty universally agreed upon by all of those who make up my strange little universe).

On our second date, we were in a cab and that song came on the radio and that's when I got the first and only rant about it from her which I was so glad wasn't instigated by me.

In that soft, sweet, and very thick southern accent of hers, she went, "That line that goes like 'two years and you'll be done with school, and I'll be making history like I do'. What a condescending, self-righteous fucking thing to sing. Like fuck your degree or diploma, I'm gonna be all huge and take care of you and it's because of you but don't miss me. If you said that to me, Jason, if you wrote in a dedication something like, 'Hey, baby, I'm so proud of you for getting your degree but don't you worry about a thing cos this book is gonna be huge and I'll be able to take care of us', I'd set your books on fire and have a friend record it and post it on YouTube."

She paused as the cab slowed to a stop at a red light.

I remember looking over at her. She was wearing a loose blue Three 6 Mafia tank top and a black cardigan and I was totally staring at her nice tits.

Then she pulled her cardigan closed and went, "Plain White Tees are fucking Plain White Boring even though they got that black drummer who ain't even playing on that song."

"It's like that band Extreme."

"Totally," she laughed.

"Their only hit song and the fucking drummer doesn't do shit."

"Remember in the video there's that shot of him standing up from the drum kit and walking away when the song starts."

"You're right. And the rest of the video he's got his feet up, reading a magazine not giving a single shit about what those two gnar burners are doing a few feet away. And why should he? Unless he got hosed on the royalties though."

"Ahhhhh. Right. What an interesting scenario. You're in a band that's got that one song and one song only. But you don't have a part in the song and for the rest of your life, people are like, 'Extreme had a drummer?' or, 'What magazine were you reading in the video?"

After that, she let her cardigan open back up and she slid over and held my hand.

Tonight, Delilah is wearing a white lace, see through dress, a pair of black cowgirl boots, a leather jacket that I bought for her during a day trip we took to wine country, which ended in a total disaster and began our insanely quick spiral to the bottom, and this sweet black felt fedora with a brown band around it.

She gives me the biggest, warmest hug, and then kisses the side of my mouth.

"You leaving or staying?" she asks.

"Leaving, babe. Ryan told me to meet him here and he just texted me that he's at Lucky 13 now so I'm going there."

This huge grin cuts across her doll face, and she goes, "I'm heading there as well."

"For the same thing?" I ask.

"You betcha. My nostrils are thirsty. It's been a week. Plus, he's got those Oxy's too."

I make a face and go, "When did you start making those your jam?"

She sighs and pouts her lips.

And me, I just wanna grab her face and kiss her so badly and tell her how sorry I am for the way I treated her and the distance, all that fucking distance I put in between us right after we'd began to get so close at my own insistence.

It was so pathetic.

Something I'm great at being from time to time.

The way I deal with the bullshit I've created all by myself, with no prompting or encouraging, just me being drunk and high (actually, me being drunk and then high on Molly, like two or three capsules, or two pressed pills, or an entire gram dumped into a glass of water, that kind of high).

It's jammed me up in so many ways with so many girls, that just thinking about it paints my face red and makes me wanna disappear from this city for good at times.

Maybe change my name.

Maybe move back home and live in mom and dad's basement in Iowa.

Maybe jump off the Golden Gate Bridge.

Not only is it embarrassing and shameful (the things I've said and done, especially during sex) but it's also hurt people, like really hurt them and I've caused them a lot of pain and heartbreak.

For instance, me proposing to Allison because "it just feels so right, baby" and "because I'm ready to take the next step which means us, me and you, together, baby and forever."

Yet we didn't even live with each other and earlier in the night, before I took that shit, I'd had a twenty minute conversation with a friend of mine about how fucking boring Allison was and that I couldn't respect anyone whose only aspirations were to wake up early five days a week and sit in an office all day and do whatever someone else tells you to do.

I told him about her painfully boring stories and how she took forever to tell them and most of them were pointless and sucked and how part of me considered her to be this giant fucking whore because she lived with a dude who paid for everything - rent, phone bill, scooter, school textbooks, trips they took, clothes, just everything - despite her claims that she hadn't loved him for the last year they were together.

But that night, I rolled hard. Three capsules plus a bunch of whiskey. And we were naked for the next eight hours and she was letting me do whatever the fuck I wanted to her and at one point, I said, *"Let's get married."*

Her face exploded with happiness.

And I went, "I'm for real, babe. Marry me, Allison. Let's do this."

"Okay," she said. "Oh my god. Are you really proposing?"

"I am. Allison, will you marry me?" I asked.

It ain't like I had a ring or anything.

Again, we didn't even live with each other and I'd refused to give her keys to my apartment and I always made sure I took my coke and my wallet with me whenever I left her in any room by herself for longer than twenty minutes.

But I felt so good.

Just great about life.

Even her story about this fat coworker of hers who went on the "Jared Subway Diet" but gained weight and her story about fixing a spreadsheet problem and getting a Jamba Juice coupon got me pumped up and really excited about her life and her career.

And then we had more super awesome sex and finally fell asleep.

It was like one in the afternoon when we woke up and she wanted to run down to the store and get a really nice, expensive bottle of champagne and some sort of fancy dessert to celebrate.

"Baby," I went. "It's just Saturday."

Her face turned white and her eyes red.

"Excuse me?"

"Here," I went, then grabbed forty bucks from my wallet. "You pick it out. It's a special Saturday, ya know."

She still seemed a little strange but smiled then put some clothes on and left.

Me, I sat up and I reached for the mirror. There were still a few lines left on it and that's when I noticed this sheet of paper with dates on it.

I picked it up and my fucking stomach turned.

The top of the page said: "Potential Wedding Months and Locations".

Goddamn it, *I remember thinking.*

Goddamn you, Jason Myers.

And I stared at the piece of paper as it all came crashing back.

Instead of doing the lines on the mirror, I fucking dumped an entire gram out and snorted the whole pile in one try.

After that, I drank the remaining half bottle of whiskey then quickly began devising my own plans on how I was going to slip out of this jam.

Everything was on the table, too.

There was no bottom to the depths I was willing to explore for an out.

This was never going to happen.

And because I knew this, I also knew that ultimately, my fate with Allison was sealed.

You don't come back from something like that.

You don't come back from a "Molly induced proposal" initiated by sexual acts, put on the table for one fucking night, and one fucking night only.

And I fully understood this.

I knew what it ultimately meant.

She was going to get fucking destroyed.

That was the bottom line.

I was going to have to destroy my girlfriend because I got too high on Molly one night and said some shit.

And the most fucked up thing about it to this day is that I swear to God, I really do, that during part of the sex we were having that led to me proposing, she looked like Kim Kardashian, and that's who I thought I was fucking for like an hour.

Back to Delilah Kaitlyn Lee now.

And I say, "You gonna answer that question?"

"I started doing them around the time me and you stopped seeing each other."

"Right around the time?" I ask.

She makes a face and says, "I took my first one the night I told you I couldn't see you anymore. Like romantically. The way we'd been for like almost a whole month."

"Gotcha."

Pause.

"Sorry," I say. "It's not like something that's ruining your life or anything, right?"

She shakes her head. "It's not."

"That's good. I pop those 30's from time to time too. When I like wake up at four in the afternoon and it's all sunny and seventy degrees out and I've missed the entire day. Looking around my messy fucking room, feeling like I don't even remember what I was trying to work on or the next big idea I had for a new book. And then I'll pop one of those things and it's nothing but beaches, flowers, and fucking rainbows."

"I'm surprised about that."

"About what?"

"You knocking down Oxy's."

"It's the manufacturing of happiness, Delilah. Just like I say in *Blazed*. Why deny yourself something that guarantees your happiness when you fucking know that nothing else you're going to do, or anyone you're going see that day will make you feel like that?"

She grins and then she takes my hands and goes, "If only you could've pitched or at least summarized your fucking feelings about us the way you just did about Oxy, who knows, maybe-"

But I stop her before she can finish her thought. And I say, "Maybe we'd made it a week longer than we did, love. That's all that would've done. Extended the inevitable for a few more days and wasted your time."

She lights a cigarette now and offers me one. I take it even though I don't feel like smoking another one right this moment.

Shaking her head slowly, she says, "I guess I still don't get what I did wrong, Jason."

"Nothing," I say.

"Man," she says back. "It sure didn't feel like nothing. Me and you, we go and we spend these two amazing nights in Monterrey. You spend the whole time telling me how perfect it is and how much you needed this and me in your life. And then we get back to the city and I don't hear a fucking word from you for a week."

Pushing a cloud of smoke out of my lungs, I say, "Yup."

"What the fuck did I do? And don't say nothing either, Jason. Don't you dare say that it had nothing to do with me, and that it was all you. Just tell me, dude. Tell me what happened."

Right as she's finishing this demand, I notice a taxi rolling up with its light on and I step into the street and wave it down. It pulls over to the side of the road.

"Are you fucking serious?" she goes. "And you're out like that?"

Taking one last drag of my smoke before flicking it onto the street, I open the door, and hold it there, and I say, "Yup. But we're going to the same place, babe. Remember? So come on. Let's roll, doll."

Her face springs back to life, and she tosses her smoke and jumps into the backseat.

Me, I take a coupla deep, deep breaths, run my hands down my face, step inside, and close the door.

Immediately after Delilah tells the driver our destination, I roll down the window and think about how amazing it was to not have to talk about anything real in Los Angeles other than how good the sex, the weather, the food, and my books were.

It was so easy there. So pretty and buzzed and totally devoid of any real responsibilities. The opposite of here.

And once again, I'm to blame for this too.

Most of my time during the peak of my popularity and financial success was spent chasing a fucking ghost and trying to figure out how to find some way back to a fucking time that gleamed on the surface and should've been enough for both of us.

I should've known better than to think those were just a couple of cracks in that shiny surface.

Cos they weren't.

They were fault lines and once they were activated, they fucking destroyed everything.

And my grand solution to this unavoidable disaster which everyone (let's not kid ourselves) fucking everyone saw coming, was to literally try and recreate some of our best days together. And when that wasn't working even though we were telling each other, smiles on our faces, that it was (I mean, we would actually go out and fucking celebrate not fighting for two days then proceed to get into a huge fight during the celebration) I'd spend hours locked in my room reading old emails from when we first got together and sometimes, I'd even go on Facebook and read some of the awesome statuses I'd written about her when we first got together.

It blows my mind.

Like, I find it pretty fucking amazing that during some of our longer split ups and breaks, there were these gorgeous, stunning, and successful women I'd meet out at shows and art openings and parties.

Women who were fiercely independent and so artistic and incredibly ambitious outside of whatever sort of day job they worked to pay the bills until their grand visions came to life.

Women who had all the great qualities that Allison lacked and who wanted to spend time with me and pursue relationships with me and were actually fucking nice to me and intellectually curious and self-made, yet all I could think about was how to go back to the beginning with Allison.

I was convinced there had to be a way to do that. To harness all that magic and happiness we once had and translate it to the present.

But it's impossible to do.

And deep down inside, I knew that it was.

I knew it was a ridiculous waste of time.

And most of all, I knew that even if we were able to somehow find a way to be together again, even if it was just a fraction of what we'd been at our best, it would've been me refusing to take the next step with her. It would've been me doing everything in my power to put some distance between us. And it would've been me lying, just like it was when we began to get more and more serious, about spending the rest of our lives together and building that cute home in the country and building that adorable family we spent so many nights lying in bed talking about building and being done with everyone and everything else.

This is the real truth and I know it.

And so does she.

It's just that she always believed that I was also in love with the actual possibility of that life.

She never knew that the only part I actually loved about that was the story.

In the cab now, on our way to Lucky 13, a bar that once had my band GrundlePig's song, "Pro Mean" available for play on their jukebox, Delilah goes, "I deserve an answer, Jason. I deserve all of them."

This fierce surge of anger suddenly tears through me and I go, "You fucking whores and your sense of entitlement."

"Excuse me?" she rips.

Swinging my eyes towards the front of the cab, I notice the driver looking concerned as he looks at us in the rearview mirror.

And I say, "It was three months ago, Delilah. Honestly. It's history. Ancient fucking history now. Why on earth would you wanna go back there?"

Delilah, she leans over to me and goes, "Because it was so much fun, Jason Myers."

She says, "It was thrilling. I remember you telling me like right at the beginning about how horrible you were at relationships and that I'd get so sick of you not wanting to spend all your free time with me. You said I'd start going nuts and losing it cos I was gonna become so insecure and unstable from always thinking that you were cheating on me when you'd decide to write instead of see me. You told me all that shit and then you said the best thing ever."

"And what was that?"

"You went, 'but even though you're gonna despise me and hate me, even though you're gonna get jealous of all the young, beautiful girls who write to me and post on my wall. Despite all of that, you're gonna love all the dinners I cook for you, you're gonna love all the flowers you'll receive, you're gonna love the sweet notes I write for you and that I'll hide around your room for you to find...which I still fucking do sometimes, by the way. And every time I do, I get so incredibly sad at first, like really, really sad, but as more time passes, the notes ultimately make me happy, Jason."

Pause.

A sudden hush comes over Delilah as she turns her eyes away from me and towards the window.

This is like so not what I wanna be talking about or even fucking thinking about right now.

Or really ever again.

Like here I am, actually fucking doing something at night in this city for the first time in awhile, chasing something I think I need, something I've convinced myself I need actually, but it's not just needed for my enjoyment of it nearly as much as it's needed as some kind of security blanket I can wrap around myself to keep the anxiety from crushing me.

And I'm chasing it through a city that's becoming more and more unrecognizable to me as more and more and more of its edges dull.

As all this history and all this past just bleeds out and begins to dry up.

And we all know what dried blood becomes.

So there ya go.

And now you've seen their plan.

Remove the stains.

Push the source out.

Rebrand everything.

It's like open heart surgery.

Remove the old one.

Replace it with a trendy artificial one.

Then claim you're the same but just better.

Instead of staying like Paris, you try to become Manhattan.

I'm chasing, chasing, chasing something that'll make me feel fucking great for a short period of time. But this feeling I'm after, it ain't one that I'll ever be able to own, that'll ever truly be mine, and the harder I fucking chase it, the easier I've made it for my past to catch up with me.

Slowly turning back to me again, Delilah goes, "You also said that I'd really love it if I was ever able to convince you to go shopping with me. You said, *'You're gonna love it when I hand you my credit card after I find a corner in a cold, dark bar while you shop. A dark bar where I'll get fucking lit and listen to the fucking Stones and Guns 'N Roses and Nirvana only. Just those three bands. And just three other important things. Tequila. Corona. And cocaine'*. And you called cocaine the only thing you'll ever really love."

I start laughing.

"And you did all of that, love," she says. "Also, you did love cocaine and Nirvana more than me."

"Don't forget about Wu-Tang and Mobb Deep."

She laughs.

Then she flips me off.

And then she nods, and says, "And lastly, you said how I was gonna love my days off with you."

"Right," I say.

And she goes, "How I was just gonna love being holed up in your apartment with a fridge stocked with champagne, and endless piles of cocaine on a mirror that I could just help myself to and not worry about wearing anything else besides my bra and underwear all day."

"And it was all true," I say.

"No," she goes. "It wasn't."

Making a face, I go, "Which parts weren't?"

"The first parts, man. I never gave a shit about you spending nights away from me to write just like I never thought you were really with another girl when you were doing that, just like I never got jealous of the young, beautiful girls who did write you and who you did talk to back. None of that bothered me. Ever."

Right after she says this, my mind instantly begins replaying every second of our relationship that contained any animosity between us whatsoever and she's right.

Not one of our arguments (I only think there were two or three all together) were about any of the shit I'd told her she'd hate me for.

Instead of any of that shit, one was about a Trivial Pursuit question and answer.

Another one was over that Don McLean song "American Pie" and her insistence that she knew what every line fucking meant then proceeded to bring up website after website dedicated to the meaning which then led me to bring up an interview where McLean himself states that all the lines are open to interpretation and that he'll never reveal what each line meant to him. Which simply broadened the scope of the argument on whether or not artists should disclose the intention of their art and its meaning or just let the audience let it mean whatever it does to them.

And the third argument was about the Double Stuff cookies I ate in her bed while she was at work, leaving crumbs everywhere and not cleaning them up before I split for the day.

That fight, the third one, also happened to be the only fight where multiple grams of cocaine and bottles of wine were not consumed beforehand.

Bored and restless from this conversation already, I say, "What sort of answer would satisfy you?"

"An honest one, I suppose. About your disappearance from my life and the way you ignored all of my attempts at trying to get a hold of you."

I'm about to answer her but stop and rethink what she's asking.

As the cab turns left and sits at a red light on Valencia, she goes, "Well..."

And I say, "How's your life right now?"

"It's great, Jason."

"And Facebook and Instagram tell me you're seeing someone and that everything you do is the best thing ever until you guys do something else and then that's best thing ever."

She laughs. "Something like that."

"And you're happy, Delilah? You're honestly, truly, just so fucking happy with your boyfriend, your career, and every fucking day you wake up is glorious because you get to live through it all and take part in another day of this great happiness?"

"Yes," she says. "This is where I'm at. This is how I feel."

"There you go then," I say.

"I don't understand."

"We rarely fought, and we did have a lot of fun, but you weren't happy with me like you are now. Like you are with him."

"That's still not an answer."

"You shouldn't need one," I say. "Let it fucking go. Appreciate what you have and how happy that makes you, Delilah, and quit worrying about why I dropped out of your life. It had nothing to do with you."

Another pause.

I bite down on my index finger and know I'm going to regret saying this next thing but what the hell, I don't care.

I might as well at this point.

Dropping my hand to the side, then grabbing hers and squeezing it, I go, "I wasn't happy."

It's like the wind's been knocked out of her. And she lets go of my hand and says, "You always seemed happy. You always said how much fun I was."

"You were, Delilah. But my unhappiness had nothing to do with you."

I clear my throat now and look away from her before going, "You were just a distraction."

"What?"

"I hated my fucking life and I was, I still am, terrified about how it's going to play out and what I'm going to do next and I fucking hated waking up most days. I fucking hated living through most days until I'd see you and all of a sudden, none of that shit mattered. That was the fun part, baby. I was happy there was someone to distract me from all the other bullshit going on in my head."

"So why fucking bail like that on me if it was helping you so much?"

"Because," I say, grabbing her hand again and squeezing it. "One of the things I've come to realize and really understand about relationships is that if one person in it is incredibly unhappy with themselves, like deeply, and terribly wounded and fundamentally sickened by things that have happened or the way things are turning out, things that began and were happening way before the relationship started, that person's issues are going to bleed all over everything and the other person won't have any idea what's happening or what they can do to help because they can't do anything to fucking help. So then your mind is going to go wild wondering what the hell you did wrong and it's going to make you fucking crazy. It will eventually turn into a disaster but even before the disaster, it'll get cold and distant and mean. Perhaps you're right, Delilah. Maybe I shoulda sat you down and ended it like an adult, but I didn't do that. I never put you through the pain and the embarrassment of begging me to let you help me through this shit I'm going through only to stand up, reject you, and leave you. I just left you alone. I didn't want you to go through what I did with Allison cos it wasn't pretty and the more I pushed her to let me in and fix her, the more she acted out and hurt me and I became a disaster too."

Delilah, she still clings to my hand and runs a hand down her face as she looks out the window again.

"And now look at you," I say. "You've got everything you want so far and you're glowing and you've got a dude who seems to think the world starts and ends with you."

"The way you always talked about it was that she was just a lying whore, Jason."

"She was."

"So you were the one pushing her away?"

"No. At least not until the end. What I've come to realize though in these last six months we've been apart is that I was just as unhappy with myself inside as she was. I was just in denial because everything I'd worked my ass off for, everything I was doing was successful and the money put a lot of band-aids over the deeper wounds. It was able to cover up a lot of my own unhappiness with myself."

The cab pulls up in front of Lucky 13 now and neither of us moves.

"Is it a horrible thing for me to want to tell the driver to take us back to my place right now and let you make love to me?" she goes.

Smirking, I go, "No. It's only a horrible thing if you would actually tell him to do that."

"Right."

I reach into my back pocket and take my wallet out and hand the driver a twenty and tell him to give me four back.

"So what do you really want, Jason? What is going to make you fucking happy?"

"I don't know yet. I still haven't figured that out yet."

"You should let me know when you do."

"What if that never happens?"

"Nothing from what you're telling me. But I'd like you to be happy, babe."

"Can you get me a guaranteed four book deal worth a quarter of a million dollars, snap your fingers and make my debt disappear, become nineteen again but still own your businesses, and make it so that I never have to leave the house for cocaine again?"

Delilah starts cracking the fuck up as the driver hands me my change. And then she jumps towards me, throws her arms around my neck, and slams her mouth against mine.

We spend the next thirty seconds making out and I even get two fingers into her pussy for a few seconds before she gently pushes me away, and says, "For old time's sake."

"If you say so."

"Would you have stood up and left if I'd done that after the conversation you didn't put me through?"

"Probably not."

"See."

"I would've stood up and left ten minutes later after I pulled my pants back up and asked you if you were still taking your birth control pills on time."

"Fuck you," she snorts. "And you end that moment by taking away anything good I felt from that conversation and that fucking story."

Following Delilah out of the cab, I go, "You've read my shit."

We both light cigarettes.

"You know I don't believe in happy fucking endings, love."

"What do you believe in?"

"Getting it right."

"Wouldn't getting it right mean a happy ending?"

"No," I tell her.

"How so?" she asks.

"Because there are no happy endings, don't you understand that?"

"I guess not."

"To end is to reach the final point. There's no existing after that. These are our lives we're fucking talking about, alright. You will never, ever get another one of these."

"No shit."

"I don't fucking care about a happy ending because I won't exist when it ends. I only wanna get it right. So that's what I believe in. Getting my story right."

13.

Lucky 13.

"What happened to this place?" I say to Delilah immediately after we walk in.

"You really don't get out much anymore, do you?"

"No," I say. "I definitely don't and I'm beginning to think I've really spared myself and everyone I woulda potentially been with a ton of snide remarks and some serious negative baggage."

"Ha," Delilah cracks.

"What?"

"Negative baggage," she says. "What a great fucking band name."

I stop walking and contemplate this for a moment then gaze across this scene. This odd mix of punk rockers, turquoise v-neck sweaters, dykes, droopy eyed bender goblins, boring girls with hair pulled back into ponytails and pre-torn jeans, frat boys in baggy jeans and khaki shorts and backwards hats.

"What do you wanna drink?" Delilah asks.

"Negative Baggage," I say.

"Right," she says.

"Great band name. And I'll have a tequila and pineapple."

When I take my wallet out, she goes, "I've got this, babe. You paid for the cab."

"Thanks."

I head straight for the jukebox. Journey is blasting from it. One of the surest ways to figure out if one of your favorite old haunts is changing from the inside out is walking in and hearing any Journey song followed by whatever mix of white trash arena rock the asshole who stuck five dollars into the box chose.

Me, I throw a five in just so my song plays next and when it does, I'll be able find the shithead who played this by scanning the room again to see who's about ready to cry into their beer.

The song I pick is "Hell On Earth" by Mobb Deep. And then I slide another five spot in and choose "Ya Know How We Do It" from Ice Cube's *Lethal Injection* record.

Delilah walks over to me and hands me my drink.

"Nice choice," she says.

"My bedtime music," I tell her.

"I remember."

"Really?"

"Of course I do, love. The first three nights I stayed at your place. We watched the sun come up from your roof with our Maker's Mark "nightcaps" we used to wash down the Xanax bar you'd break in half. Then you'd stretch and I'd watch you knowing that you were about to turn around and ask for my hand so you could lead us to your room."

"What is wrong with me?" I just blurt out, after slamming my drink, and identifying the cliché, I mean person, whose plastic trip down memory lane I just blew to ruins with my favorite Mobb Deep song.

Bitch looks barely twenty-one.

And her jeans are like bell bottom cuts. And she's wearing a gray sweater with a purple vest over it. Her hair is plainer than I'm sure her personality is. And she's talking shit to her chubby friends about me and rolling her eyes.

Delilah shrugs. Then says, "Nobody knows, Jason. I thought we established this in the cab."

"Oh yeah."

I set my empty glass down on the table next to the jukebox. "You remember everything don't you," I say, not ask.

Nodding, she says, "I remember most of it. You'd lock the door and slide your comforter down so I could crawl in after getting undressed. And then you'd put this record on and crawl into bed with me and lean against the headboard and I'd drape my arm over you and we'd get stoned while you'd tell me about some new story idea that you were kicking around that day."

She goes, "Even then, Jason, stoned and drunk and exhausted, the passion in your voice was exhilarating. Your love for stories and characters, the way you'd quote Jim Harrison and Raymond Carver and Hemingway, it was contagious like, dude."

She says, "And then you'd drop some random ass story in about being on Ketamine at The Regency backstage with the dudes from 400 Blows and smashing a bottle of beer in front of the sound engineer from The Butthole Surfers and screaming, '*Kanye West is the only God I pray to, Nigga!*'"

"Oh, Jesus," I say, blushing now, and running a hand over my face. "And there's no way I could talk you into breaking up with your man and giving us another try?"

She takes a sip from her straw. "I'd listen."

"Really?"

"Sure. But that's as far as it would get."

"Why even bother to listen then?"

"Are you fucking kidding me?" she goes. "I don't know what that conversation would be like but I imagine somehow you'd mention a Melvins show you saw once, a car you took a joyride in, hitting on Grimes in some bathroom once, and the floor plans you drew from your memory of some bank you wanted to rob after you'd been up for three days. That's why I'd listen."

Delilah saying this, while it's sweet of her, and mostly true, and it comes from an honest, sincere place, it also makes me cringe inside and want to disappear, which normally I'd be able to fucking do, just disappear into the ladies bathroom and slam chunks of blast into my nose but I can't cos this asshole with the drugs hasn't been anywhere he's said he'd be and I don't see him anywhere in here. And going into the ladies bathroom without coke is definitely not the same as going in there with it.

You're just a fucking perv at that point.

You're like worse than the bro with the white, unbuttoned polo shirt and spiked hair, who fucking cat calls at girls as they walk by him before jumping back into these intense and loud sports arguments he gets into with his buddies who'd be down to film his sexual assaults on their phones.

Having coke with you though, all of a sudden there's a single file line in front of you and you're passing out the potential of a drip that will change the flow of an entire evening.

You're getting phone numbers handed to you on paper towels. And anything you have to say or wanna say, any story you feel like sharing, quoting something from

Zerzan's anarcho-primitive essays or completely validating the Ralph Nader/Matt Gonzalez, 2004 Presidential ticket to someone who's never voted before, is being devoured by these chicks because that's how much they want a taste of this stuff they swear they never fucking do.

And you tell them, "I saw fucking Pearl Jam on the Rock The Vote tour and it changed my life. My next tattoo is gonna be this huge back piece of Eddie Vedder jumping from the balcony into the crowd in the "Alive" video."

And they're gonna love it and ask you where they should get their work done cos they've finally decided on which Bright Eyes lyrics to get tatted on them.

It's a remarkable difference.

And the reason I wanna run away is because Delilah is too real and too sincere and knows me too well after just that short amount of time we spent together.

While me, *fuck*.

Me, I don't even remember if she lives with roommates, the name of her dog I used to take for walks, or if she has sisters or brothers.

Staring Delilah dead in the eyes so intensely she looks almost timid now, I lean over and put my hands on her face.

"You need to know this, okay?"

"Relax," she says, without even attempting to brush my hands away. "My man is going to be here any second."

"Just shut the fuck up and listen to me."

Her mouth closes but her eyes slide towards the floor.

"You're better than me. You're a better person than me. You're nicer, you're sweeter, you're more pleasant to be around, you're positive, you're not vindictive, you're not petty, and best of all, you'll never sink. There will never be an undercurrent strong enough to pull you down. You are everything I'm not and then some. You're fucking beautiful, and why you were ever fucking me is something I'll never understand. And in the end, I'm glad we had what we had and that I get to live the rest of my life having experienced that. But once again, you're better than me. And whatever else you do and experience

going forward are things that wouldn't have happened if
we had stayed together."

"You're being way too hard on yourself."

"No," I say. "I'm being honest. New experiences
with me are like learning every single lyric off the *Ready
To Die* record after staying up with me for a coupla days,
playing marbles with the tour manager of Nine Inch Nails
at the Brown Jug at six a.m., and taking a cab less than
half a block to buy a six pack of Miller High Life and a pack
of Camel Crushes."

Once again, Delilah's laughing hysterically, and
I've still got a hold of her face.

"Thank you," she says next.

"Thank you," I say back, as "You Know How We Do
It" starts bumping. "One more kiss?" I ask.

This time however, which is what I really wanted
to happen, this time she says, "Nope, no more of that
shit."

She knocks my hands away.

She blinks.

And then she looks to her right and goes, "My man
just walked in, Jason."

She points towards the door and I painfully look at
this fucking chowder head.

This pilgrim dick.

Delilah's new man.

Her big Instagram show off.

The man Facebook tells me she's with all the
fucking time.

Dude's like 5'7. He's skinnier than Delilah. He's got
scruff all over his face and huge bags under his eyes. His
light brown hair hangs down to his shoulders and it's kinda
styled messy on the top while his bangs are cut straight
across his forehead and hang down to his eyes.

He's wearing a jean jacket with a yellow Trans Am
t-shirt underneath it, stone washed, boot cut jeans and a
pair of white Chuck's.

I can't help but start laughing out loud. Like I ain't
surprised, I guess, cos I've seen photos of him and her.
It's just seeing it in the real is so much different and shit.
Seeing the guy who dresses and vaguely looks like he

wants to be the non-existent, never was, sixth member of the Dead Boys standing across the room gives the pictures (which were the jokes) their punch line.

"Better fucking go then," I snort, still laughing.

"Don't be an ass," she says. "Come over and meet him."

"What does he do?"

"He's unemployed right now."

"So what does he do?"

"He plays music. His band, Tiny Diamonds, has a show next Tuesday at Neck Of The Woods."

"How old is he?"

"Thirty-six."

"What time does his band play?"

"Why?"

"Cos maybe I wanna go."

She makes a mean face at me, before going, "Nine or nine-thirty."

I start laughing even harder now because I feel way better.

Of course this dude's world starts and stops with her (whenever he wants it to start and stop with her). He's an unemployed musician whose band is opening some shitty bar far enough out in the city for no one to go to which means she's probably paying for everything, giving him money, and he's got all the time in the world to spend with her.

"What's so funny, Jason?"

"So it's you that's buying all that Roget I see you guys drinking in the pictures?"

"Jesus Christ, dude," she snaps. "You're totally right. I ain't nothing like you. Jealous and full of envy."

"Delilah," I go, as she's starting to walk away. "Hey."

I even grab her arm.

When I do, I look up and see her dude staring at me. He's scowling and probably wondering if I'm still fucking her or if we've already fucked tonight.

I know this dude prolly better than he knows himself. I've been in bands with this guy. Robbed bricks of cocaine from dumb motherfuckers with this guy. Snorted the tiny chunks of cocaine this guy found in the carpet of some band practice studio floor at six in the morning.

This guy is also fucking anything else he can when Delilah's not around. He's using her. Say whatever you wanna say about me but I've never used a girl for anything other than sex and when I say that, I mean that it's been a mutual use. One night stand shit. But never, ever, ever, have I or will I ever fucking date a girl for a place to crash. Date a girl so I can get fed. Be with a girl to get clothes and drinks and jewelry and drugs. Like fuck that. Like in the pictures, I just thought this dude was dressing a part he was barely pulling off.

But seeing him in the flesh now, looking into those soulless fucking eyes (that were always hidden behind sunglasses on Instagram) this dude's only ambition with Delilah is to use her for everything I just mentioned and whatever else he can squeeze out of her.

Part of me is furious because she's way better than him just like she's way better than me. She deserves to be the one getting housed, fed, and showered with gifts and good sex (I guarantee that dude doesn't fuck her properly) and whatever else she fucking wants.

But another, much bigger part of me, really doesn't give a shit that she's with a dude who's taking advantage of her. From what she's told me about her exes during our brief time, most of them were dudes in bands whose bands weren't doing shit.

Totally unsuccessful.

Totally lazy.

And totally full of themselves.

"Welcome to the San Francisco music scene," I remember saying to her one night as we were leaving the Elbo Room. We were there to see some band whose name I can't even remember and whose set did nothing for me nor did it do anything for any of the people I talked to while I smoked cigarettes outside. Yet when I went back in to get Delilah, climbing those stairs that can be so unforgiving at one a.m. after seven or eight Corona's and three or four tequila shots, she emerged from the "green" room (which is the size of my bathroom), and took me back there to meet the band.

The bottom of their nostrils covered with cocaine residue.

Shades covering their eyes.

Jean jackets, leather jackets, and ripped jeans.

Only two other girls besides Delilah were with them and those girls were only unforgettable because of how beat they looked and how much they kept fucking yapping about how great these dudes' music was and how they were going to be bigger than the Libertines one day (seriously, one of those dumb bitches actually said this).

I remember the dudes talking as if they'd just sold out the fucking Warfield or something despite there being maybe a hundred people at the show.

As if somehow, attracting an okay sized audience to a decent club on a Friday night was some sort of a partial guarantee that a record deal wasn't too far away in the future despite them having no touring plans and despite them having no records for sale at the show (just a handful of CD's) and when one of them finally spoke to me (and he only spoke to me after he noticed a bag of cocaine in my hand) he asked me what I thought about the set, and I was like, "That Motley Crue cover you guys did sounded alright."

And he went, "Oh cool, man. Thanks."

And I went, "It sounded like you guys memorized the song riff by riff and played it like they would've."

"Totally," one of the girls said. "And that song is like, one of the ones that's really hard to do that with."

Sidenote: *The song was "Girls, Girls, Girls".*

Anyway, so yeah, this dude Delilah's with, who probably spends more time on his hair than she does, this is the dude she's fucking now and supporting, but she's happy, and I'm not.

So who fucking cares anyway?

"What?" she snorts.

I'm about to talk shit but it's just not worth it and it just doesn't matter, like it really just doesn't, so instead of pointlessly laying into him or her, I say, "He makes you laugh."

"Yes." She smiles again and this lightness returns to her.

"Alright," I tell her. "Do the honors, love."

"Thank you, baby."

"You're welcome, D."

Then I wink and shove the two fingers I jammed up her pussy earlier into my mouth.

A smile as big as the ocean emerges across her face and I wink again while Mister Dead Boy cardboard cutout glares at me even harder.

Been there done that, brah!

And here's hoping my dick is as delicious as Delilah always said it was.

14.

Oh, and by the way, Ryan, he's not at Lucky 13 anymore. The text I get says he's at the Hemlock now so he can see this great fucking SF band, Little Teenage Black Girl with Bella, his twenty-eight year old girlfriend who used to be a fairly successful model (you've seen her in *Inked, Maxim, Vice, American Apparel, Spin,* and *Rolling Stone*), and now she writes for *Vogue* and *Vanity Fair.*

She's 5'10 and she's got this gorgeous long brown hair that hangs all the way down to her ass.

Every inch of her body from the neck down is covered with ink (and Ryan's confirmed that the "every inch" part is very, very true). Her body is so sleek and slender. Her lips are thin. Her eyes are the kind that you'll fall in a deep well for. And she's fucking smart.

She's the fucking girl that brings every room she enters to a halt, everyone stopping what they're doing and shutting the fuck up and taking a moment to get a real nice look at her.

She becomes the envy of every girl.

The desire of every man.

Delilah's gorgeous.

Allison's beautiful.

But Bella is both of those.

And then she's stunning on top of that.

Ryan, he's a good fucking sport about it, too.

Actually, fuck that, he fucking cherishes and adores the attention Bella receives whenever they're out together. And why wouldn't he fucking cherish and adore it?

He's receiving almost the same amount of attention because of it.

He's the envy of every single fucking man in those rooms.

And he's the object of every single woman in that room's curiosity as they wonder what's so fucking special and great about him.

Why is she with him when she can have whoever the fuck she wants to have?

Cocaine and a mutual infatuation of Carcass and Faith No More are the main reasons I've come up with.

And good for him for reveling in that and loving that.

I've known so many guys, friends of mine, who actually get all pissy and agitated when they go out with their pretty hot girlfriends and see guys checking them out.

That's fucking awesome.

Why would you ever give a shit about that?

You have what they want.

This is something to celebrate.

Not something to get angry about. And be a shit to your girl for looking that good.

But I know dudes who are like that and it's so fucking ridiculous.

That kinda insecurity.

That sorta misguided anger.

And all of them, the dudes who are like this, all of them, they front like they're some kinda badass. Front like they're so fucking cool and shit.

Yet they have a meltdown when they think too much attention is paid to their babe.

It's so ridiculous, totally gross, and insanely telling about themselves, who they really are, which goes totally against the perception they're desperately trying to portray.

Anyway, dude ain't here no more and I'm really beginning to get irked with him. I'm able to place an order for a Dewar's and soda right before meeting Delilah's new man.

Keith Jim is his name.

And like, that's really his name, too.

I've been assured this twice since I shook his hand fifteen seconds ago then watched Delilah and him kiss twice. Both times her eyes sliding to the left to make sure I was looking.

"Did you get Ryan's text?" I snort. "He's at the Hemlock now."

"I know," she says. "Are you going?"

At first, I shrug. But then I look around me. And nothing that I'm looking at is appealing to me whatsoever.

And I tell her, "Yeah. I think so. Plus, it'll be good to see Little Teenage Black Girl play."

I grab my drink off the bar.

And Keith, he goes, "So you're the writer guy."

"What does that mean?" I ask him.

"What?" he goes.

"What's a writer guy?"

"Like you write and stuff," he says.

"I guess. Doesn't everyone though?"

He shoots a look at Delilah and then Delilah shoots a look at me, and I say, "Sometimes I write books, man."

"I write music," he says.

"I'm sure you do," I say.

Swinging my eyes back to Delilah now, I say, "Are you gonna go?"

"To where?" Keith Jim snorts.

Right as I'm about to answer him though, Delilah takes it upon herself to answer his question and then my phone buzzes.

It's another text from Allison.

And it reads: *I can't take this, Jason. This birthday sucks compared to last year's. I've changed so much, ya know. I really have. And all I can think about is you tonight and how I fucked everything up. I know I did some really bad things. I know I hurt you. And it makes me sick to think I could do that to someone I loved so much. Who I still love. But I've changed, baby. I have. Please call me. I wanna find a way to see you tonight. I wanna find a way to get back to us.*

The only thing this text does is make me even more angry about her and what happened to us.

Like you've changed, bitch.

Really?

You wanna tell me you've changed and expect me to believe you have cos of a text you sent to your ex-boyfriend while you're with your new, current boyfriend.

Like give me a break.

Fuck you.

The only change I'm seeing is that it's a new guy, this flute guy, being the sucker in your games instead of me.

Pounding my drink in one huge gulp, I go, "So, you guys wanna go?"

"We're good," Delilah says. "Keith's got some shit on him."

"My shit," he goes. "And hers but nobody else's."

"Awesome."

"We're gonna head to the Tiger Kill," she goes. "Last night, ya know."

"Right," I say.

Keith wraps his arm around her waist and kisses her again and then the two of them, they just walk out and leave me standing here all alone.

After I delete Allison's text, I walk outside for a cigarette, trying to figure out my next move.

Sliding a smoke in between my lips, I text Ryan back that I'm coming to the Hemlock like right now, and then I light my grit and watch Delilah and Keith fucking Jim jump into a cab up the block.

Leaning back against the side of the building, this absolute like total fucking feeling of overwhelming isolation and alienation takes ahold of me.

My anxiety slams into this super intense mode and it's nearly unbearable. Totally uncomfortable.

Me questioning what I'm doing.

Not only here but with my fucking life.

Unable to smile or communicate with strangers.

Unable to answer a phone call from anyone other than my dealer.

Unable to feel confident about the future except in rushes of adrenaline that happen maybe a few times a day and barely last a couple of minutes.

And with their conclusions arrive the same doubts, uncertainty, and lack of life clarity that precede them for hours at a time.

"Titty Coke," I hear again.

This pulls me out of my funk and I look up and see my homie, Dan Daisy rolling down the block, paper bagging it.

"Hahahaha!" he goes. "Mister Montana. What the fuck are you doing?"

"I don't know," I tell him, then start walking towards him.

"I never see you out anymore," he says.

"I'm out sometimes."

"I ain't seen you out in at least a year. Probably longer than a year."

Shrugging, I go, "So what. I'm out now. It's good to see you, man."

"You too, Titty Coke."

Me and this dude, we go back like twelve years and shit. Dude's like my height. He's got a curly blonde afro. Black framed glasses. Some sick tats on his back and chest and stomach. And he's wearing a pair of tight black jeans, a pair of baby blue KED slip-ons, and a navy blue American Apparel hoodie.

"You here by yourself?" he asks.

Pointlessly looking around, I go, "I am. Now. Well I was. But now you're here. But before that, I was with this chick Delilah."

"The babe that's dating Keith Jim," he goes.

Rolling my eyes, I go, "Sure. But she was dating me before him."

"Chick's so hot."

"You know her boyfriend?"

"Yeah. I see him here and there. Total dick but sorta fun to be around."

"Cool."

"His band sucks though."

"Whose band doesn't?" I snort.

Dan Daisy laughs and goes, "So what's up? You going to the Tiger Kill?"

"Yeah. At some point. About to head to the Hemlock though to meet Ryan and grab something."

"Awwwwww," he goes. "He's not here?"

"Nah. He bailed with Bella, I guess."

"Fuck. I went all the way out to the Knockout and got the same shit."

"Me too," I say.

"Here," he goes, handing me the brown sack.

There's a pint of Jim Beam inside it.

I take a huge pull and hand it back.

"I'm about to catch a cab down to the Hemlock if you're down," I say.

"I guess," he goes, looking past me at all the other smokers. "It ain't like this place is happening."

"Nope."

Right as I say this, all this yelling and shouting starts. It's coming from inside the bar.

Glass starts shattering.

It sounds like a table gets flipped.

Girls are screaming.

Dudes are yelling.

Girls are yelling.

Boys are screaming.

And then this load of like four skater kids, and like four Marina hipster, techster, broster dudes spill onto the sidewalk.

Punches are flying.

A skateboard smashes against this dude's head.

A knife is pulled.

Two chicks are kicking this dude who's unconscious on the ground.

"Fuck this," says Dan, then darts to the curb and hails a cab. "Yo, Titty Coke," he says. "Let's bail."

"Yeah."

We jump into the backseat and I'm still smoking and I go, "Polk and Post. The Hemlock."

"No smoking, sir," the driver says. "Not in this car."

"Sorry," I say.

Rolling down a window to throw the grit out, I go, "Hey! Assholes!"

Two of the dudes in the brawl, one from each side, they both turn and look at me.

And I say, "Both of your bullshit scenes ruined the Mission."

I flick my smoke at them and roll the window back up.

15.

"So what's new with you, man?" Mister Daisy asks as we near the Hemlock.

"Besides this new book coming out, nothing. I have no idea what's gonna happen when this thing is released and nothing else lined up."

"You mad about that?"

He passes me the whiskey and I go, "Mad? No. Scared as hell...yes. I mean, I've got no money coming in, man."

"Really?" He goes. "Cos the last time we kicked it, you made it seem like you were mister money bags. Daddy fucking Warbucks and shit."

I take a pull and laugh. "I mighta been embellishing a little bit, dude. Like, I was set at the time. But now, my royalties from the first two books are nothing like they were and *Dead End* and *Run The Game* haven't started earning royalties yet."

"Happens, I guess."

I take another pull. "Apparently it does."

I hand him back the whiskey and he goes, "I just assumed, with the way you cut yourself out of every fucking social circle these past coupla years, that you had a fucking library ready to throw at the world. I mean, nobody ever sees you or talks to you anymore. I hear things sometimes but that's it and shit. Usually from Ryan. We're all under the assumption that you're building this fucking empire."

Squeezing my forehead, I go, "There were some projects that never happened, ya know. I thought I could write anything and sell it after the first two blew up but I was wrong. Then I had to write *Blazed* to get some dough and that's all I got. The money from that came and went. Me and Allison are done for good. I never see anyone anymore. And it's all my fault. I fucking isolated myself, man. Like, bad. I mean, I really alienated myself from everyone I came up with here. It's just so strange..."

"Whatcha mean by strange?"

"Like having the success I've had. I remember when I was writing *Exit Here* and I thought, I fucking really believed, man, that just getting one book published would be the fucking shit and I would have no problem doing whatever else for the rest of my goddamn life. And now, it's like I don't want anything else. I can't do a nine to five, man. I mean, I can. Like literally and physically, but it'll kill me inside. I can't go back to that shit. I can't. But it's looking like I'm gonna have to cos there's nothing else coming out, dude. *Blazed* is it."

Dan Daisy hands me the whiskey again and goes, "Fuck that, dude. You'll think of something else."

"I've thought of a lot of other things, dude. Tons of other crap."

I take another swig and force it down my throat.

"Truth is, I'm just a mediocre writer, man. I've got some huge ideas that I'm incapable of carrying out. And I ain't even got any friends no more."

"Oh you still got friends, man. You got a ton of friends left. All you gotta do is call us, homie."

The cab pulls up in front of the Hemlock and I pay for it and the two of us get out.

"This motherfucker better be here," I say.

"No shit. But if he ain't, we still gotta kick it, ya know."

"True."

"You can still have fun before you get the bag, man. Not everything good comes after the coke."

16.

The Hemlock.

Me and this bar, we've got so much fucking history together.

And prolly if I'd spelled my name with cocaine on this bar, if I'd nailed some gorgeous girl I had no business nailing in the girl's bathroom here, this would be my favorite bar in San Francisco and not the Tiger Kill.

However, my overall history with the Hemlock is better. The seminal shows I've seen here: Replicator opening for Big Business. Triclops like four fucking times. The Fleshies at their peak, their prime, their end, like all at once. One of Get Dead's first acoustic shows. Thrones. The Richmond Sluts. Victory & Associates. The Blind Shake. Vaz. Coachwhips. The Cat Power surprise show during Noise Pop two years after I moved to the city. And Mount Vicious.

My first glass set in San Francisco (six stolen pints) came from this bar. Two of the four girls I woulda dropped everything for on the spot, no questions asked, and done anything they wanted me to do for the rest of my life, I met here at Punk Rock Monday over a decade ago.

And I also got into my first San Francisco fistfight at this bar like four months after I moved to the city. It started in the smoking room. *Me approaching this tiny Asian girl I'd gone on two dates with two months earlier.*

Apparently, our brief conversation came across as too flirtatious to this fucking meathead she was seeing.

After I hugged her for the second time, he got right in my face.

"Who told you you could hug her?"

I smirked.

"I asked you a question," he barked.

"Relax, homie," I went. "You're the one who gets to fuck her."

She laughed. And he shoved me.

"Dude," I snapped, as I stepped back towards him. "Not cool, man."

The girl, she just backed away. And when she did, her place was taken by two of his friends.

You can stare into another man's eyes and tell if that man is going to punch you. Staring into his eyes, I wondered if he could tell I was going to hit him first.

I held my hand out for him to shake and when he grabbed it, I decked him in his right eye with my left fist (always lead with your off hand. Always. Doing that allows you to use the initial shock whoever you just decked is reeling from to come back with your strong hand and land the more serious blow).

I delivered the second shot to his kidney.

This is when his friends joined the show.

Unfortunately for me, I was there by myself that night. The whole thing lasted less than two minutes. I got worked pretty good. Two black eyes. A broken nose (which I snorted coke with an hour later back at my crib before typing a ten page screenplay about a hooker who slices the throat of a John she thinks robbed her best friend). And a busted fucking bottom lip.

These are the things that you should never forget. Never, ever, ever.

The important stuff, I guess. Like glassware, pussy you'd ruin your life for, and swinging your fist into the kidney of a douchebag with your strong hand.

17.

Anyway, it's packed in here which does nothing but agitate my anxiety times a hundred.

Since I paid for the cab, Dan Daisy fucking braves the crowd hovered over and around the bar, wedging himself in somehow to get a great spot.

Me, I text Ryan that we're here, then look around and don't see anyone I even know so I figure they've all gotta be in the back room where the live shows are.

Like two minutes later, Dan hands me a shot of tequila and a Corona. I dump the shot down my throat and me and him, we head towards that backroom.

I actually sorta know the door guy. About a year ago he was at my crib raging with a bunch of fools. Around seven in the morning, the last of the fools left, or so I thought.

I went out to the roof to have one last cigarette and when I walked back into my room, this dude was passed out on my floor. I didn't really know him that well. He came with some friends of mine I hadn't even seen in like over a year. So after failing to wake him up for like ten minutes, I texted one of the guys he came with to get his address. After that, I called Yellow Cab and when the car arrived, I fucking picked this dude up and carried him down the stairs and laid him onto the backseat before giving the driver a hundred dollar bill pasted with cocaine.

Little Teenage Black Girl has already finished playing, which sucks. And once again, Ryan is nowhere to be seen. So I slide through the crowd and make my way towards the backstage.

Raymond, the front man for LTBG, is standing next to the stage covered in sweat.

He's wearing tight black jeans and a white Crosses t-shirt and he gives me a hug.

Me and him, we go way back. I've known him for at least eight years and we've been pretty tight for the last five. Two years ago, I even went on the road with his previous band, Conflicted, for a quick Southern California tour and wrote an article about it which received over ten thousand reads on my website.

"Did you see the show?" he asks.

For a second, I think about lying to him and telling him that I did before deciding to be better than that.

For once, recently.

Just be fucking better than that.

"Shit, man. I just fucking missed it. I just got here."

"Fuck," he goes. "It was our best show to date. Easily."

"I'm sorry, man. I just got back from L.A. today. Been a crazy few nights."

"I bet."

"You seen Ryan at all?"

"He just left," says Raymond.

"Fuck!" I snap. "That cocksucker."

"Chasing the bag tonight," says Raymond.

"Something like that," I say. "Being a fucking amateur."

"Come on back," he says, as the headlining band, Bleeding River, begins to sound check.

"Cool."

I look around and don't see Mister Daisy anywhere.

Fuck him.

And then I follow Raymond back into the tiny ass green room of the Hemlock. Immediately, my eyes land on this girl, Melanie, who I dated for about six months before Allison.

She looks better than ever, too, which sucks because she looked so good when we were together. But I fucked up that relationship big-time even though, up until about a year ago prolly, I blamed her for its dark, ruthless demise.

Melanie has long black hair. Her septum is pierced and she has these sharp green eyes. Two huge, golden, oval shaped earrings hang from her ears. She's wearing a white dress with black stripes wrapping around it, black stockings, a pair of black flats, and this dope leather jacket I bought her from a thrift store in the Mission on our third or fourth date.

Which consisted of us getting stoned at Dolores Park and drinking tall cans for like three hours with some of her homies who I never really took to all that much.

Then I bought a bag of coke from some skinny hipster in the alley next to Delirium. After I shoveled nearly half the horribly stomped on bag up my nose in the bathroom, I told her I wanted to go shopping and that I'd buy her the first thing she saw that she'd ever love more than me.

It took her about five minutes in the first store we walked into before she was wearing that jacket.

Melanie also fronts this electro-pop band, Sleeping Beauties, who are actually blowing up right now and that does make me a little envious but whatever.

Her face lights up when she sees me.

"My favorite author is here...no way."

I roll my eyes. "Bullshit. You still ain't read a single word I've ever written."

"Not true," she says. "I read most of those like ten page texts you'd send me at five in the morning about whatever random shit the cocaine convinced you was really important. Like the choose your own adventure book about the drummer of Def Leppard and all the endings have to do with him losing his arm or not. Or if that scene in *Wall Street* when Charlie Sheen gets arrested and cries as he's being taken out of the office in cuffs was basically foreshadowing his life spiral to the bottom. And my personal favorite-"

"Okay, okay," I go. "You made your point. You've read my shit."

"Well this one was special because I got it fourteen hours after you stood me up and I hadn't been able to get a hold of you."

I sigh. "Fine."

"You were giving me your credit score numbers over the years and explaining what each of them meant and your current one at that time you claimed meant that you lived in a two story house and had a wife and one point two kids and two point three pets."

She goes, "But when I called you like immediately after you sent the last one, again you didn't answer. Then one afternoon I got really bored and decided to look up those scores myself and they were actually terrible, like really, really fucking bad, terrible. And that's when I knew the real reason you didn't have a credit card."

I'm blushing.

I don't say anything back.

"Jesus, Jason," she snorts. "Relax. I'm not saying it to be mean."

"Right."

"Oh, come here," she says, holding her arms out.

Now, I can't stop myself from grinning.

"Bring it in," she goes.

"Alright," I say. "You smell nice."

"Thanks, doll," she goes.

"What are you doing here?" I ask. "I'm surprised you'd be at this show."

"I'm friends with Richard," she goes. "The drummer in Little Teenage Black Girl."

"Oh, sweet."

"Did you see the set?" she asks.

Shaking my head, I say, "Nope. Missed it."

Leaning forward, I whisper, "I actually only came to find Ryan."

"He just left."

"I've been told."

"He said he was going to the Tiger Kill."

"Really? That's where I wanna end up."

"Me too," she goes. "I loved that place."

"We all fucking did. I hate what's happening to this city."

"We all fucking do," she goes.

I pull my phone out and check the time. It's just past one. There's also two texts.

One from Ryan that says he's at the Tiger Kill.

And another one from Allison that just says: *Jason, I'm dying to fucking see you or at least hear from you tonight. Please...*

I put my phone away and go, "You serious about heading there for last call?"

"Totally."

"You with anyone else?"

"Nope."

I grab her hand and go, "Let's bounce then. Come on. I'll pay for the cab."

For a moment, Melanie seems reluctant. But she gives in because she has to.

Because it's me.

And I know she still adores me even though she started to fucking hate me about three or four months into our relationship and then hated me even more after I cribbed this short story and made fun of her band.

"Come on," I press her. "We're going to the same place."

"You're right," she finally says. "You are right, Jason. Plus, there's something of yours I still have and wanna give back to you."

"What?"

"You'll see in a minute," she goes. "Let's get out of here, babe."

A whole night, I'm thinking, spent with ex-girlfriends who were nice to me only to have me treat them like total shit.

And the only girl I treated like a fucking queen treated me like a piece of shit.

But now she wants to kick it, while these other girls, they're only kicking it because I've run into them.

It's a bizarre turn.

This strange fucking life.

These chicks are rad.

Maybe I treated them so poorly cos I knew they were better and cooler than I'll ever fucking be.

Who knows?

We look for the Daisy man.

Neither of us see him and his phone goes straight to voicemail.

"Fuck it," I say. "We out."

"Yeeeee!"

18.

"So what's this thing of mine you wanna give back?" I ask Melanie after informing the cab driver of our destination.

Melanie starts laughing.

I've always loved her fucking laugh too.

I loved Melanie a lot.

She's the first girl in San Francisco I said I loved and honestly meant it.

This was back in 2008.

Melanie starts digging through her Chanel purse.

While she does, I begin to think of the proper way to tell her how sorry I am for the way things ended up between us.

I was so selfish.

So fucking shitty.

"Here it is," she goes, holding two folded sheets of paper in her hand.

"What the hell?" I go. "Love notes?"

She laughs again and says, "No. You never wrote me any love notes, Jason Myers."

"In my head I did," I say.

"Well thank you for that," she says.

Right as she's about to unfold the paper, I reach out and grab her arm.

Melanie looks up at me. "What's up?"

"Listen," I start. "I just want you to know how sorry I still am for the short story."

Melanie pulls her arm away and goes, "I know you are. Everyone in the band knows you are. It's fine."

"And about us," I continue. "I've never had the chance to tell you this face to face."

"Jason-" she starts. But I stop her.

And I go, "I was a fucking wreck when we were together."

"No shit," she says, the words drenched in sarcasm.

"I think a lot about what would've happened if we'd found each other a year later or fuck, even six months ago. It would've been so different. I would have been a great fucking boyfriend."

The cab slows up for a red light.

And Melanie goes, "But you were a good boyfriend for the most part."

"No I wasn't."

"Yes," she says, taking my hand now. "You were for long stretches at a time but then there'd be this distance you'd put between us and you'd just detach from me and your life became off limits. Those pieces of time did hurt because I never knew why it was happening and you'd never talk about it and you'd show no interest in me and what I was doing. It made me feel like I wasn't at all important to you. Even though I knew somewhere in the back of my head that I was, it just never felt that way. It just felt real cold and helpless."

"I was really fucking selfish. I know. About my time. And I wasn't happy with my life in general."

"And all the cocaine too," she says. "God, every night I saw you, you were high."

"Yup."

"And it totally affected our intimacy. Sex is important to me, Jason. It really is. And we were fucking like two, three times a week and that's it. That's bullshit. I kept telling you that it was fucking things up but all you wanted to do was get high and talk shit."

"Fuck," I snap. "I know this, Melanie. I was an asshole."

"Don't snap at me," she goes.

"I shouldn't have even said anything in the first place," I shoot back, as the cab begins to accelerate through the intersection.

This sharp, awkward silence follows before Melanie finally says, "I'm glad you did actually."

"So you could beat me up even more."

"No," she says. "I'm glad you did because it's coming from a place of sincerity. Anytime you apologized for flaking on me or being real moody and distant all day, I never felt like you really gave a shit that it'd happened. Your apologies always seemed so contrived, like you were doing it because you had to, which you did have to, but that was it. Never because you were really sorry for any of it. So this is nice, Jason. Cos I know you mean it and I know you're a different person than you were when we were together."

"Thank you," I say.

"Thank you," she says, before leaning towards me and kissing my lips.

I get a boner immediately as I kiss her back. But when I slide my hand around the back of her neck, she pulls away and says, "Let's not get carried away now."

I grin. "You started it."

"I always started it with you. I had to. You'd be so high and going off on all these rants. Just so consumed by all this shit that had nothing to do with anything that was even affecting your life."

"Whatever I was saying, I'm sure I thought it was pretty important."

"Duh," she says. "Isn't everything a little more important on cocaine? Everything except shit like responsibilities, telling the truth, and listening."

"Think you just nailed that pretty good," I say. "So what the fuck does it say on those sheets of paper? I'm dying to fucking know now."

"I don't even know why I've kept it in my purse for this long. I guess maybe cos it's so awesome and that I thought it might come in handy with your insane lifestyle."

"What is this?"

"Your will," she says.

"Come again?"

What she said, those two exact words, they startle the fuck outta me. Even the cab driver seems startled by what Melanie's just said.

"My fucking will," I snap. "When...how...on those sheets of paper?"

"Yup," she goes. "In your own shitty handwriting which is barely fucking legible. But I've deciphered it."

"When did I give this to you?"

"About a month before I quit talking to you. Right around the time I was reaching my fucking breaking point. You were supposed to meet me out for drinks at the Hemlock, actually. My sister and some of my homies from L.A. were up here visiting and I really wanted them to meet "the author" but you never showed up. Remember?"

My face turns red. I do remember my disaster now. Not the details by any means. But the fallout from it and that sinking, gut wrenching feeling that I'd finally broken her back.

"You went to see *American Psycho* earlier that night with that guy, Billy Billz or something. Then you said you were gonna roll to the Hemlock but never did and I didn't hear from you for over sixty hours. That's when I decided just to show up at your crib unannounced and found you laying on top of that white bearskin rug in those ridiculous Naughty By Nature shorts. And next to you was a mirror with four seventeen inch lines on it which I measured myself. I was in awe. From that and from the insane amount of empty baggies surrounding you."

Like three heart piercing, chokehold-like images of that bender smash through my head as she tells the story.

And I feel sick.

This makes me sick.

And I almost tell her to stop talking about it until I realize how petty and unfair that would be to her.

Like not one bit.

Not one tiny ounce.

"Fuck, Melanie. Again, I was a total wreck, a fucking shitshow even though I acted like I had my shit together all the time and talked about how much harder I worked than everyone else. I mean, you know. You were there."

Pause.

"Sometimes," I say. "Sometimes you were there. But a lot of it was bullshit. Just a show I was putting on. That I'm still putting on all the fucking time. Every single fucking day. These masks I'm constantly wearing. It's like I don't know myself anymore. I'm conflicted all the time."

"About what?"

"Everything, Melanie. The things I want out of life. The purpose of this day to day shit and what it even means to me anymore. I can't even tell you where I want to be in a year and even if I did know, I certainly don't have any clue on how to get there right now. It's so crazy. This fucking fall from grace I've had. I just..."

My voice fades now and I take a deep breath.

"Go on," says Melanie.

"I don't know what happened."

"Jason."

"It just disappeared," I say. "Poof. My world vanishes, my life erodes, and instead of figuring any of this out, I'm chasing a bag of cocaine through the streets of San Francisco because that's about all I know how to do anymore. I know how to get high. I know how to disengage. And I know how to stay isolated."

"I thought you liked being alone."

"I do," I say. "But being alone and being isolated are two very different things and somewhere along the way, that line fucking blurred. This isn't alone I'm doing. It's isolation."

"Not tonight," she says.

"No," I go. "Tonight, too. I just bumped into you at a bar. Just like I bumped into Delilah earlier and Dan Daisy and Keith Nightmare and some dumb bartender who thought the worst show my band ever played years ago was amazing. That's just fucking bizarre to me and sorta retarded. Why the hell would you even remember that?"

Melanie starts laughing again.

And I say, "I love your laugh so much."

"I know," she says. "And you've always been able to make me laugh."

"What do you think I did more of? Piss you off or make you laugh?"

"Huh," she sighs. "You made me laugh more. Easily."

"Really?"

"Sure. But the way you pissed me off had way more of an effect on how I ended up feeling about you."

"And there you have it," I say.

"And this," she says back. "I still have this."

"Jesus."

"When you gave this to me, I'd just gotten to your place and we went into your room and you told me to sit down and you lit a cigarette. The booze was just peeling off of you. Then you kneeled down in front of me and took my hand and you were like, '*You're the third sexiest girl*

I've ever kissed, Melanie. Do you wanna know who number one and number two are?' I told you no."

"Obviously."

"And then you ripped these two sheets of paper out of a notebook, folded them, and told me that if anything ever happened to you, this is how you wanted all of your life divided up. And I was like, *'You wrote your will?'* and you said, *'Not really. I started this about two hours ago but that's not the point'.* Then you held this out and asked me to please take it. That it was the least I could do since I'd been being so tough on you lately."

Even the fucking driver is laughing now as Melanie opens it.

"Are you going to read it to me?" I ask.

"Do you want me to?"

"You might as well. You fucking kept it in your purse for all these years."

Giggling, she goes, "Oh, it's so good, too."

"I bet."

"Miss," the driver says, as we hit another red light.

"Yeah."

"Would you like some light to help you read?"

"That would be wonderful," Melanie says. "Thank you so much."

She flips her eyes back to the top page and giggles some more.

"Well go on," I snort. "Let's hear the will I wrote for myself four years ago."

"Alright," she goes. "Here it is, Jason."

And then she begins:

Well, right before she begins actually, she goes, "Besides your handwriting being god awful, your spelling is atrocious, too."

"I know," I say. "It fucking looks like a retard with Tourettes got busy on some paper."

"Yeah," she says. "If this had been four pages instead of two, it wouldn't exist anymore. No way could I have tried to go through another page of this. Especially not two."

"Come on miss," the driver blurts. "Read the papers. Please. The will, read it."

"Settle down up there," I snort.

And Melanie, she says, "No, he's right. I'm reading this thing right now."

And then she begins.

But for real this time.

She goes, *"As you're all well aware of by now, I'm dead. Please don't be mad or sad about this. You're all gonna die one day too. I just did it first. Just like I was the first one of any of y'all to own every N.W.A. cassette tape. The first one wearing white KEDS to school. The first one to finger bang Racheal Rathmussen's gnar puss. The first one to think James Franco is actually a really good actor...good actor at least...but I think "really good", that was me saying that first...I think...Maybe...But I'm pretty sure I was the first Franco fan overall. And I said something about him being good first. That's what I do know. And I was the first one to cry when Kurt Cobain killed himself. He told me. I was on a ton of acid and had just smoked DMT. This is when he told me I was the first and I believe that to be true.*

"So yea, please don't be mad or sad right now. Or ever again. I wasted too much time of my life being angry. Like what does it really matter that you think Dave Eggers is brilliant?

"What does it matter if you think Lose Your Illusion 1 *is a brilliant album? And what does it matter that you think Aronofsky is a better filmmaker than Paul Thomas Anderson...I mean it's bullshit and not true at all but really, what does it matter.*

So don't be angry is the point.

Sometimes it's okay.

But try and also let some things go."

Melanie pauses as she slides the first page under the second.

"Oh wow," I go. "Not even front and back."

"No," she says. "Just two front sided pages."

"That's so weird."

Looking back up at me, she goes, "Yeah, that's it. That's totally the weird part out of all of this. You not going front and back."

The driver laughs and I go, "Since you're getting such a big kick out of this, mister driver man, how about you let me smoke a cigarette in here."

"Go ahead, sir," he says, and even rolls the window down for me.

"Thank you."

I light the grit.

And Melanie says, "*I forgot to mention in the opening that there should be a box of tissues in the room where this is being read in case anyone is crying. Or has to blow their nose cos they've been partying lately and doing too much cocaine and their noses might be stuffed. All of this said now (well written) here it goes.*

"*I bequeath all of the money in my savings, checking, and wallet, and if anyone goes through my jeans or pants or jackets plus any loose change in the room, to my mother. I love you so much, mom, and I miss you and I still owe you for the garage door and van repairs from when I backed the mini-van through it three years ago on my way into Dysart to get cigarettes and then lied about it.*

"*I believe there's about eight hundred dollars in both accounts and at least a floating hundred in other various places mentioned above and there might be a few fives hidden in a sock that I've been trying to find for the last week and a half. Now music (this is super important). All of my cassette tapes should go to my oldest sister, Adriana, because a lot of them (at least the ones from before 1995) are hers. My CD's now. This is more tricky. Anything that can be defined as metal, post-punk, hardcore, post-hardcore, punk rock, post-new wave, industrial, and noise rock/post-noise rock should go to my dear friend, Allen, who burned most of them for me after those three CD cases of mine were stolen from a house party I threw last year. And whoever stole them has a special place in hell, too. So not cool, bro. Any CD that can be defined as hip-hop, gangsta rap, R&B, post-R&B, Motown, and electronic should go to Melanie, my lovely girlfriend who hates me and has every reason to but hopefully now that I'm dead, she won't. The rest of the CD's are for the house cos I'm pretty sure a lot of your guys' CD's are in my collection now and if I said I didn't*

have it but you find out that I did, it wasn't that I was
lying to you as much as I didn't wanna go through
everything and look for them.

"Posters now. This is a huge deal cos they deserve
to be on the right walls, hung with pride by those who will
appreciate them and have always tried to get them from
me through various means. Trades for cocaine. Trades for
concert tickets. Trades for two High Life 40's (really Keith
Nightmare?).

"And a trade for a dope Eazy E baseball cap that I
sorta wish I'd done now that I'm writing this. Anyhoo,
here's how the posters on my wall should be divided up:
The Ghostface Killah/Big Doe Rehab, The Faith No More
poster for The Real Thing, and the Jesus Lizard poster
signed by David Yow's best friend should go to former
bandmate and one of my best friends, Murray K.

"The Guns 'N Roses Lies poster should go to my
brother in law, Kale (dude's the first person I ever heard
say Lies is better than Appetite For Destruction and then
follow such a bold ass statement with some very valid
points even though I ultimately disagree). Poster's his.
Plus he used to always lift weights in the garage while
listening to G 'N R and I was a better person for witnessing
that a few times a week when I was 17. All the posters
from the shows my bands played in SF, those should go
into a museum eventually. I'd like Mom to hold onto them.
I signed all of them. Some museum should want them
someday and if none do, then fuck all of the curators in
the world and dedicate a corner of the garage in the house
I grew up in by hanging them there. And the four Cage
posters, the Fab Five one, and the Camu Tao one should
go to my boy, Ricky. He's the one who bought me the Fab
Five documentary and he's the one who played that Camu
song "Wireless" for me first and that song changed my life
for a year. It's the second reason behind Cage's "Agent
Orange" that I started my second band. And lyrically, I
don't think there's a better fucking song than "Wireless."
Shit's gold. So is Ricky. And so are those posters. All my
motherfucking posters are gold, yo!"

Melanie glances back up after reading this last part and says, "Your posters are pretty dope. I've always liked them. Sorta bummed I don't get any."

"You got enough posters on your walls already," I snap back. "Plus, I hooked you up with tapes."

"I gotta lot of those, too."

"Do you want me to change it?" I ask. "I'm pretty sure I can still."

"It's okay," she goes.

"You sure?" I say. "Doesn't sound like it is."

"It totally is," she goes. "I'm sure your weightlifting brother in law will be stoked."

"Me too."

Pause.

I take a drag.

"At least he better be."

The cab pulls up to a stoplight on Mission and 16th.

Melanie makes a face and says, "It doesn't even feel the same."

"I know."

"How the fuck did time move so fast?" she goes. "How the fuck did we watch this shit change and do nothing about it?"

"What the hell were we gonna do?"

"I don't know," she says. "I just know we did nothing."

The light changes.

Looking back down to paper, Melanie says, *"My clothes. I don't care what you do with them. But just make sure all my Mobb Deep tees and Lighting Bolt tees are never worn again. Please fold those and put them in a drawer somewhere and never open the drawer again."*

Nodding, I say, "That makes total sense."

"And finally," she goes. *"My books. All the rights to the printed ones should go to my family. Start a trust with the royalties or something. Or maybe take a few fucking cruises. Money is yours. Someone should also go to Paris and rent a flat for a month with some of the dough. God knows I talked about doing that enough, but obviously I never did. And as far as the million stories that are saved*

on my desktop that I started but never finished and all my notebooks, please cremate those with me. They are my ideas. That's my imagination. Those are my dreams that never came true and since I can't dream anymore, they should end with me...P.S. I know I always claimed that T-Boz was my favorite TLC babe but that was a lie. Left Eye was the one I wanted the most. Any bitch who's willing to burn down a mansion to prove a point is my kinda bitch. Maybe I'll hit that shit in heaven. Now that would be some sweet shit...Double P.S. I apologize for my handwriting. Disaster spelling, meng! And I'm out!"

The cab driver, he seems underwhelmed by the ending of my will, which is different for me. The reaction, I mean.

Since I began writing books, I've only been accustomed to people being completely overwhelmed with my endings. I watch him shrug his shoulders before he turns the light back off.

Like, whatever.

Like, piss off and shit.

And me, me I'm like experiencing this really sinking, cruel, deflated sense of purpose in my life. Even though that was written on a bender and even though I was out of my mind when I was writing it, my entire life's worth fills up two front sides of lined paper and that's it.

I mean, there is something very liberating and satisfying about having little to nothing. Not owning shit you don't need. Not having your life weighed down by items that take up space, items that need attention which eats away at the small amount of time you do have while you're here, items that come with bills at the end of the month.

It's this truth that Palahniuk wrote about in *Fight Club*. When he wrote, when Tyler Durden says, "The things you own end up owning you."

And he's right about that.

He totally is.

And for thirty-one years of my life, this was something I consciously tried to adhere to. Something I was always very aware of. Plus, I'm pretty fucking low maintenance. I've never needed a lot of shit.

Never, ever, ever.

But something's changed over the last year. And I'm not exactly sure what sparked it, when the evolution really became an evolution that turned my world upside down.

It's not that I need or want a lot of things as much as it's that I wish I had some nicer shit, I guess.

There are some days when I wake up around four in the afternoon and the whole day is gone. Vanished. It's like it never existed. And I'm covered in sweat. My sheets are drenched. My body hurts. And I'm so goddamn depressed and sad.

I'm alone.

I have nothing and no one and it's starting to hurt more and more. As I begin to concentrate, obsess almost about the things and the life I don't have instead of being proud and focusing on the shit that I've done and have coming out.

Like *Blazed*.

That book is incredible. It's so fucking fierce and so fucking honest. The characters pop, they're so alive and so fucking passionate about life and art and what they're doing and want it to become.

It's fucking rad.

It's my best book by far.

Yet here I am. Here I've been. So close to welcoming my fifth novel into the world. And I think about it maybe once every couple of days, maybe even less than that even though it's so fucking good.

Better than any of the other books.

It's just so bizarre.

And hearing Melanie read this will in like two minutes, I don't know, I've never wanted much but I thought there'd be more to give away by this point.

Rubbing my chin, I say, "Alright."

I take a deep breath.

"Thanks."

"Are you okay?" she goes.

"Yeah."

"Jason," Melanie starts. "It's funny."

"I know."

"It's ridiculous and insane and it is what it is. But now you look so sad. Your eyes and your face..."

Her voice fades and she doesn't finish this thought.

The cab stops at a red light at the intersection a block away from the Tiger Kill.

I see at least forty people standing on the sidewalk out front and in the street. It looks like a block party and it should be one.

Swinging my eyes back over to Melanie, I go, "I'm not sad. It's just empty. My life..."

Pause.

I take another deep breath and go, "Somewhere down this road I took, my life became empty even though everything I'd always wanted to do and accomplish was being done and being accomplished."

"It's your fault," she says.

I bite down on my bottom lip and nod.

And Melanie goes, "We all watched you do it. People have talked about it with me. Once you started dating that square looking bitch and your shit started blowing up, nobody saw you anymore. You withdrew. I'm not close to you, Jason. I'm not actually sure I was ever that close to you even when we were together. But it's sad to see you like this. You've got four fucking books published. Two of them are best-sellers and your fifth one is about to come out and you think your life sucks because you don't have as much money as you used to."

"It does suck."

"So that means you can't have fun and come out. When you were with that girl and you had all that money, were you having fun?"

"Sometimes."

"With her?"

"Sometimes."

"When did you have the most fun during that time?"

I sigh and look out the window. "Probably during the times when me and her were split up, actually. And I'd go fucking crazy. I'd actually hang out and go to shows and stay up for days. I even remember this one afternoon when me and Ryan took all this Molly and built these two dope Lego pirate ships, then I split and had dinner with these three babe friends of mine who I hadn't seen in months because Allison hated them so much. We got really wasted and then I went back to Ryan's and me and him took mushrooms. For some reason, he had a fog machine in his room too and he turned it on but something malfunctioned on it and the whole house filled with this thick fucking smoke and we couldn't turn it off."

"Did you unplug it?" she asks.

"Like an hour later we did. That's when the shrooms started kicking in. It was wicked. You haven't lived unless you've ingested at least an eighth of mushrooms and like three pressed Mollies. It was like some *Field Of Dreams* meets Hunter S. Thompson shit. And I just wanted to walk through the outfield and into those rows of corn. I just wanted to kick it with an attorney. Then one of his roommates came home. She was with these two dudes who had all this face paint on. They were coming from this theater party and Ryan totally freaked. He thought those dudes were Juggalos. I've known that guy for nine years. He's into some pretty twisted shit. There ain't much that instills fear into that man's heart, but apparently Juggalos do."

The cab starts moving again. Melanie is laughing pretty hard. And I'm going, "When his roommate and her friends walked down the hallway, he grabbed me. He was shaking and sweating. I saw tears starting to form in his eyes. I asked what was wrong and he said, *'They're here to kill us cos I talked shit about them on Myspace.'* I told him that was wrong. Like not even close to being right. And then he went, *'Distract them. Then tell them that I left.' 'What are you going to do?'* I asked him. *'Hide,'* he said. I asked him where and he pointed to under his bed. When you're dealing with someone like him, who's normally irrational and paranoid, you really just have to let the situation play out. So I told him I'd do that and then he pushed me out of his room, shut the door, locked it, killed his lights, and crawled under his bed. Like I could hear him doing it. I could hear the bed shifting and him groaning and cussing."

The cab stops in front of the Tiger Kill.

And Melanie goes, "So what happened?"

"His roommate had like two bottles of Johnny Walker Black and a case of Heineken, man. So I went to hang out with those guys."

"And he just stayed under his bed?"

I nod. "He did. And I was tripping my fucking balls off, Melanie. I was so fucking high. And I couldn't stop laughing because I knew that he was just as high and he was fucking stuck underneath his bed, thinking he was hiding from these Juggalos...who, by the way, washed the paint off their faces like five minutes later."

"Did you ever knock on his door and tell him it was okay?"

"Nope."

"Did you text him at all?"

"Nope."

"Hahaha."

"I was there until about six in the morning and then I bailed and caught a cab home and passed out. A few days later, I was talking to this stripper, Candice, that he was fucking at the time, and she told me that one of his bandmates had to take an axe and break down his door and then lift the bed so he could finally get back out from under it. I believe it was at least a day and half after I left when they did that."

"Oh my god," she goes. "Jesus. That fucking guy."

"I know."

"And this is what you've detached yourself from, Jason. Life. Stories. The shit you can't make up as a writer, you can only know it by experiencing it."

"It is."

"I ain't saying every night should be like that. No way. But still, you're not even giving yourself a chance to have nights like that anymore."

"Melanie," I say. "For two years, I spent the majority of my nights watching *How I Met Your Mother* reruns and listening to this girl I thought I should marry talk about how good her spreadsheets were getting. I listened to her debate herself out loud about whether or not she should get Human Resources training or go to law school."

"Cos you were choosing-"

"And by ten," I continue. "She would be hammered and that's when she'd get real nasty and mean and bitch about how broke she was. How she didn't have anything anymore, and her clothes were all old, and how she used to take like five trips a year but hadn't taken any in over a year, which was all just a really obvious, passive aggressive way of saying she missed not having to pay rent, missed having someone to buy her tickets to leave the country, missed being able to eat out at fancy restaurants every night, and missed having a great excuse to not go after what she really wanted because when everything is already being handed to you because your face is pretty enough to get that kind of shit, what's the fucking rush? There's no sense of urgency when you're cashing other people's checks, ya know."

"So come back, man."

"It's hard though."

"Why is it hard?"

"Cos I'm thirty-three, Melanie. Thirty fucking three and I'm starting from scratch again. That's hard. Plus the city is starting to blow. It ain't like it was seven years ago. I go to Dolores Park now and end up listening to some dumb twenty-two year old talk about all the free drinks she gets at the Beauty Bar but doesn't even know about the fucking closet with the ladder that leads to the club house in that place. Those days are gone. Those kids are gone. And now it's just some fucking tech jock with a moustache who talks about Dave Eggers like he knows him and refers to that song "Take My Breath Away" as the song from *Top Gun* and thinks Berlin is just a city he could see himself really loving one day."

Melanie opens up the door and I take my wallet out. Before she steps outside though, she folds my will back up and shoves it into her purse.

"You're keeping it?" I go.

"Yes."

"Why?"

"I'd rather remember the insane cokehead who wrote this, who treated me like shit, and who took limos to see a special midnight showing of *Lost Highway* at some crappy theater before he made it big than the cokehead I'm with now. Who doesn't even have any coke and would rather dwell in the misery of everything he thinks he lost instead of enjoying himself at all and the company he used to love before he cut them out of his life then had the balls to wonder what happened to everyone and "his" city."

After she says this, she slams the door shut and I pay the driver, and for a second, right as I'm about to get out of the car myself, I think about just telling the driver to take me home, calling Allison, having her come over, and getting drunk enough to convince myself that me and her can start all over again.

Be brand new.

Make it last by saying it will enough times.

That last gasp kinda shit.

19.

The Tiger Kill is out of booze. The Tiger Kill is so packed inside that they're not letting anyone else in. Ryan's inside the Tiger Kill according to like four different people standing outside who are also here to see him. I walk around the corner and light a cigarette and spend the next five minutes wondering why I even left L.A.

I know at least twenty, maybe thirty people standing outside of the bar and I don't want to talk to them because I don't want to talk about my books and the trips I said I was taking on Facebook that I never took and I don't want to ask if any of them have cocaine and stand there for ten minutes while they talk about whatever without even having attempted to take their bag out.

My phone starts ringing.

It's Allison. I don't answer it and when the call finally goes to voicemail, I open up my pictures and flip through all the ones I took of Natasha in her underwear last night but then close them when I remember how I told her a year ago that I'd move her up here and we'd get a place together and I'd pay for her school.

That was when I was mixing dilated into my cocaine.

The best fucking high a person can ever fucking get.

You only feel super amazing.

That's how it fools you.

By tricking you into believing in the happiness.

Which leads to the plans and promises, all that ambition created by cocaine, which aren't even remotely achievable in the time frame you've set yourself.

I mean, I just got so high I ended up conning myself along with her and whoever else wanted to talk to me if they had the misfortune of running into me.

Allison calls again.

And again, I don't answer it.

Instead, I smoke another cigarette then walk back around the corner right as four cop cars pull up and throw their spotlights on then order us all to disperse.

I call Ryan. He doesn't answer. I call him again. Still no answer. And this is when I'm done. This is when I tell myself it's over because it is. There's nothing here. This place is gone. These people are gone. And I'm alone.

Then I start walking away. I head towards Mission because it's easier to catch a cab there and this is when Allison calls again.

This time, I answer it.

Why the fuck not?

"Hey," I say.

It's so loud where she's at. It's always so fucking loud where she's at. Even when, according to her, she wasn't out.

"You're really gonna do this?" she hisses.

"Do what?"

"It's my birthday, Jason."

"I know."

"You don't even fucking care, do you?"

Here's another thing about Allison, in the massive list of other things about Allison.

Just go ahead and throw reason right out of the fucking window after she's been drinking. Actually, fuck that. Don't even let it through the door.

It's pointless.

Useless.

It's like your buddy who keeps saying that he knows someone who has a truck you can use when you're moving, yet you've moved five times since you became friends and you've still never met his buddy or seen that truck.

Don't waste your time.

What I learned about Allison while we were together, and it's not any kind of learning that really matters or applies to anything or anyone else in the world, but I learned that when she's hammered and making huge mistakes like this, like calling and texting her ex-boyfriend to hang out on her birthday while she's about to move in with her current, flute playing boyfriend, I learned that you gotta go straight for the guts. No cute dialogue. No explaining yourself. No answering a loaded, pointless question like the one she just asked.

None of that shit.

I don't often treat my time as precious, but I do when I'm involved in this type of a moment.

"Well…" she goes.

"You have a boyfriend, Allison. Go be with your boyfriend."

"I've been with him all night. He's boring. I don't wanna be with him anymore. Can I come over?"

"Don't ruin your life cos you're drunk," I say.

"Jason," she goes. "I need you. I want to be with you. Please," she begs. "Let me come over."

As she's saying this, my phone, it starts beeping.

Pulling it away from my ear, I look and see that Ryan's calling me.

Shit!

Even though I hate her guts and know this would be the stupidest thing to ever fucking do in the world, I really wanna see her too. And fuck her. And fuck her some more. And try to recreate something, some kind of awesome night we had once even though I know it's nothing more than a mirage. A physical daydream.

It's like the anti-relationship beginning.

The cruelest joke a person can play on themselves.

"Jason," she says again.

And I go, "Let me call you back."

"What?"

"I'll call you back, Allison. Please. I just need to do something real quick."

"And there he goes again. Mister writer, mister big-shot, and all his time for everything else except his girl."

"Five minutes," I press.

"Fine."

"And you're not my girl anymore."

Click.

I pick up Ryan's call.

"Yo, dude," he says. "Where are you?"

"Where are you, man? I've been fucking chasing you all night."

"I'm leaving the Tiger with Bella. Where are you?"

"I'm down the block on the corner of Mission."

"Holy shit," he goes. "I see you."

I look up the street and sure enough, there's Ryan and the beautiful Bella, holding hands and walking towards me.

I hang up.

Light another cigarette.

And a few seconds later, the man I've been chasing all night is standing right in front of me in a black blazer, a black Carcass t-shirt, tight black jeans, and black leather boots.

His blonde hair is short. Parted on the top and shaved on the sides.

"What the fuck, man?" I say. "You can't stay somewhere for longer than twenty minutes. Half the fucking city is looking for you."

"Think I care," he goes.

"Clearly you don't."

"What are you doing right now?"

"Going home."

"Fuck that," he says.

"I don't even know if I wanna do coke anymore."

Both him and Bella start laughing.

"What?"

"Three cabs with their lights on have driven by since we've been standing here. Of course you still wanna do coke, dude."

I take a drag.

Bella winks at me.

And Ryan goes, "There's a huge fucking party on 17th and Capp. Let's go."

"Fuck that."

"Fuck you," he goes. "You have me. I'm right here. Let's go to the party. It's the official Tiger Kill after-party and all of our friends are going to be there."

"Friends, huh?"

"They still adore you," he goes. "Come on."

"I see a cab," says Bella, pointing down the block. "Lights on."

Ryan grabs my arm. "Dude. You're coming with us. You have nothing better to do."

"How do you know?"

He laughs. "Cos it's two in the morning and you're standing alone on this corner talking about going home."

My phone buzzes.

Another text from Allison that reads: *Please, Jason. This is your last chance. I swear. I will never fucking talk to you again if you don't let me come over.*

Maybe it's the fact that I will actually be getting cocaine tonight. Maybe it's the fact that the way Allison's acted tonight, everything she's done, all of it, the sickness that exists in her head, that has to exist for someone to pursue something like she's pursuing while she's with her boyfriend, the man she's about to live with.

And maybe it's because I've always liked arriving to parties or bars with Ryan since he's the fucking guy with the shit that everyone wants and he likes me best cos I'm the author and writer that everyone knows and thinks I'll help them get their shit published.

Maybe it's all that plus the fact that I get what I want after getting what I wanted all last night and morning in L.A.

But when Bella winks at me again, I say, "Alright. I'm in."

Then I step off the sidewalk and flag down the cab and the three of us get in for the seven block drive to the party that takes less than one minute.

Which Ryan happily pays for.

20.

The alley that is Capp Street is fucking loaded with people.

But familiar people.

And amazing people.

Pretty people.

And some cool motherfucking people.

A lot of whom I haven't seen in years and I love it. I'm in love with what I'm seeing. Plus, this particular warehouse and me have a history that goes back to my first year in the city. This is the warehouse where I saw my first punk show in San Francisco. The Angry Amputees and The Grannies.

I cut my teeth in this city with those bands just as I did with the Tiger Kill. To this day, I know that me coming to that show that night changed my entire life. I mean, just changed the trajectory of it.

The three of us, we get out of the cab and I light a cigarette immediately and then Ryan, he grabs my hands and sticks two grams into it and says, "You owe me nothing, man. Sorry about the goose chase. There are just so many golden eggs I had to lay tonight."

I start laughing and give him a hug.

"Also," he whispers into my ear. "There's a dilated in each one, baby. They're not crushed so just know that when you are pounding it out."

"Damn, man. Thank you. Just the way I like them."

"You're my boy, man. This shit, me and you, it's blood."

"True dat."

We fist bump and Bella goes, "Enough with the *Boyz 'N The Hood* bromance, dudes. Let's go inside. Sheer Mag just started playing."

"Sheer Mag's fucking playing?" I snort.

Ryan grins, puts an arm around my shoulders, and says, "Till four a.m. We're sending the last remains of the Mission radness, the last vestige of its glory days out in style, dude."

Then he pulls me with him, past the doorman who just nods and lets us in, past the chick at the table taking the cover charge who just nods and smiles too, and down the stairs where the show is happening.

And it's all so brilliant. It's so crammed and hot and sweaty. And it's full of all the kids who made the city and the Mission so cool during those years from 2002-2009.

Immediately, I bounce to the bathroom. Locking myself in the stall, I grind down a dilated with the coke.

Dump some out on the back of the toilet.

With my debit card, I make one line that's at least ten inches. After that, I roll up a hundred dollar bill and snort it.

"Fuck yea!" I yell, as I step out of the stall and see like ten dudes I've totally partied and listened to Guns 'N Roses and the Talking Heads and The Stooges with until sunrise during those years I just mentioned.

I don't even check my face for residue.

Fuck it.

At the bar, I order a shot of tequila and a Corona and then I slide towards the back of the crowd and begin watching Sheer Mag just kill it.

Just destroy.

This is when I turn to finally look at this girl standing a few feet from me.

She's fucking gorgeous, too.

She really is.

And she's looking at me. In fact, she's been looking at me since I began standing here.

I could feel her eyes turning back onto me every few seconds.

I smile and she smiles back.

She looks Latin, which is rad, because I really love Latin girls.

Her long black hair is braided and she's wrapped some of them around the sides of her head and tied them together in the back.

A soft, yellow sundress covers her body and white slip-ons cover her feet.

Oh, and both her arms are sleeved, too.

After trading looks again and then again, she finally walks up to me.

"Hi," she goes.

"What's up?"

She shrugs. "Not much. Just having the best night of my life."

"Yeah," I go. "It's pretty good."

"I'm Carla," she says.

"Jason," I say back. "Nice to meet you."

"Right."

I'm relieved when she turns her head away from me.

I'm fucking nervous and shy and I'm totally blowing it. I need to do something right now.

Fucking anything.

"Hey," I go. "Can I tell you something?"

She swings her head back around. "Sure."

"You're fucking beautiful," I snort.

A smile as wide as the sea parts her face and she says, "Thank you. You're a babe too."

I blush. "Thank you."

Pause.

I take a deep breath.

"So what do you do, Carla?"

"I'm a grad student at Berkley."

"Nice. For what?"

"Creative writing."

My heart starts racing.

There's a lot of sweat pouring out my palms.

"That's so cool. Are you from here?"

Shaking her head, she goes, "No. I'm from L.A. My father works for MGM. He's a studio executive."

Taking another deep breath, I say, "That musta been some sweet growing up."

"It was the best," she says. "What about you? What do you do?"

"I'm a writer."

"Oh."

Pause.

"What do you write?"

"Books," I say. "I've got four novels out with Simon & Schuster, two of them were best-sellers, and a fifth one coming out really soon."

"That's my dream," she says.

"It's a nice fucking life," I say.

"Did you always wanna be a writer?" she goes.

"I don't know."

"Was there something else you always wanted to be?"

Pause.

I don't answer at first because I'm watching all these amazing fucking people dance and smile as they fall in love with the moment again and again and again.

This is the first time I've seen all the kids who made the Mission the Mission, all the real hipsters, the real art kids, the real DIYers, all of them together in the same room again since that first Knife show at Slim's in 2005.

It's perfect.

There's nothing more I could ever want out of a scene.

Looking back at Carla now, I say, "Ya know, I always wanted to be James Morgan."

"Who's that?"

"He's this dude in some of my books."

"Okay."

"He's like a best-selling author who gets to do whatever he fucking wants. He does drugs all day, drinks all day, knows everyone, gets into any show for free, and he fucks this beautiful Latina girl, Caralie in my second book, *The Mission*."

Carla's giggling.

"And that's what I wanted to be. I wanted to be him."

Stepping closer to me, she goes, "You've got coke on your face."

"Whatever."

Grinning from ear to ear, she goes, "I saw you bust past the people at the desk and walk in for free."

"Yea," I say. "It's cool."

Sliding even closer now, she goes, "There were like four people who play in bands that I cherish, dude. That I adore. And I watched them like urgently push past people and almost run some of them over just so they could say hi to you and shake your hand as you were walking towards the bar."

I make a face at her and go, "I know what's happened since I got here. I'm well aware that I paid nothing to get in and have done coke already and who I've seen and said hi to. What are you doing right now? It's fucking creepy."

"San Francisco," yells the girl who fronts Sheer Mag.

Carla wraps her hand around mine.

"You're amazing tonight! We love playing here."

Then she squeezes it, leans into me, and kisses the side of my mouth before going, "Jason."

"Yeah."

"I think you did that."

"Did what?"

"James Morgan," she says.

"Come again."

"You are James Morgan," she says, then kisses me again.

And I kiss her back.

And after all of these years of writing about it, I finally understand what James Morgan was saying, and how right he was.

About life and what it means.

"Life is about accumulating a group of stories so rich and interesting that they'll serve you well beyond the time that whatever career you have has ended. That's what this day-to-day shit is really about. The accumulation of amazing stories and having the bruises and scars to show for them," he says in The Mission.

This is the point.

To live awesome and to never stop living your life.

I get it now.

My life is amazing.

But I've been taking it for granted.

And my stories are the reason why my life kicks ass.

I am James Morgan.

This is my fucking life!

And I'd never fucking trade it.

Not even for a kilo of coke.
Or a fucking hand job from Grimes.

About The Author:

This is Jason's second novella. He also has six novels out, including two best-sellers, exit here & The Mission. He was born and raised in Iowa but has lived in San Francisco since August 2002. In 2015, he founded exit here media. His favorite band is The Replacements. His favorite album is *Let It Be*, the one by his favorite band. His favorite movie is *Buffalo '66*. And his favorite book is *Play It As It Lays* by Joan Didion although his bible is *Fight Club*.

Visit exit here media to read tons more by Jason for free as well as a slew of awesome pieces from contributing artists.

www.exitheremediasf.com

73309303R00073

Made in the USA
Middletown, DE
13 May 2018